The Bi-Word
Copyright©2014 Barry Lowe
ISBN 978-1-909934-80-1
Cover art and design by Dawné Dominique

Published by
Lydian Press 2014
Find us on the World Wide Web at
www.lydianpress.com

THE BI-WORD

Three Tales of Bisexual Romance

Barry Lowe

Lydian Press

CONTENTS

All previously published as individual eBooks by Lydian Press

Double the choice but just as hard to find true love.

THE GROOM CLOSET

The last place on earth – in the universe – I wanted to be was at a wedding. Jake, my boyfriend of fifteen years, had held on as long as he could to marry me but in the end the insidious cancer claimed him before the state changed its marriage laws to allow – get that word? – allow two people of the same gender to legally tie the knot. I will never forgive the legislative bastards for that. To rub salt into the wound the very day we cremated Jake I'd received an invitation to a wedding. What perfect timing.

The invitation came with another sting: it was from my estranged daughter. Yeah, you heard that right. I have a daughter. An accident. A combination of too much liquor and a persistent female admirer on prom night. Almost nine months to the night, a caterwauling miniature of her mom entered the world and never gave me a moment's peace until I fled from the town where everyone minded everybody else's business but their own – to the city where I was engulfed by the sweet embrace of anonymity. There was no way I was going to be trapped into a loveless marriage even for the sake of a child. I was gay; I'd known it for years, inexperienced though I was. Hell, I was only eighteen. I had wild oats to sow and I'd never get the opportunity if I stayed in Breederville. Nah, not the town's real name, but I'll use it to protect the identity of the guilty parties.

I could understand Melinda wanting to mate with one of the most eligible young men in town. I'm quite a catch. No point in being modest. I cut quite a figure back then, and still do today. I don't look thirty-eight. I'm a good-looking cuss and I've kept my jock physique although these days it's courtesy of the gym rather than through the pursuit of sporting interests, although Jake and I used to play tennis with friends on the weekend. You'll understand, I hope, that I haven't much felt like it over the past six months.

Half a year in which I've not given any thought to that wedding invitation that I shut away in a drawer along with the cards from acquaintances who felt the need to send Hallmark condolences rather than make the effort at attend Jake's funeral. He wouldn't have minded; he found the whole tradition macabre. In the end, though, his sense of the ridiculousness of it all defeated even him; the pain almost unbearable. He knew there was nothing but eternal darkness once the lights inside his body were extinguished so we couldn't even claim the small comfort of meeting again in some sort of heaven or even hell. Death was final.

Jake begged me in his last days not to grieve but to grab life by the balls while I still could. In fact, he recommended I grab as many men by the balls as my fist could manage comfortably. He could be as sentimental as the next bastard when it came to our relationship but, with the end in sight, he absolved me of the guilt of finding a new man to share my life. "You need someone, Rich. You won't make it on your own. Just be happy that I won't be in pain any more. And I'll shuffle off in the superior knowledge that you'll never find anyone half as good as me again." He laughed at my shocked reaction until his face grimaced in pain. He was being brave for my sake. We'd been together long enough that we knew each other inside out.

Our friends tried to help me in the weeks after Jake's death but I needed more than sympathy; I needed intimacy. Jake was right. Even though I sought hugs and kisses in saunas and from bar pick-ups, they were never up to him. The guys may have been better looking or better built or had a bigger cock, but it made no difference – the pleasure was transitory and mechanical. Except for the one occasion. Oh, how that boy wriggled his way under my skin. A fine looking lad, probably ten years my junior. Solid body, good mind – he wanted to discuss more than cock size and who was going to top (we took it in turns) – and a keen appreciation of the world around us. Inexperienced – very – but a quick study. I pegged him as a virgin but he admitted to a little college experimentation.

We'd met in a bar. I was going stir crazy at home and thought a little friendly bar chatter would help ease me back into the gay gene pool. It was five months since the big event and I had mentally given myself a year to shake off the blues. Not that I would ever forget Jake, but life did have to go on and I didn't want to be a miserable moping bastard to my friends. I'd neglected them of late because there was always that inevitable question, "How are you coping?" Much less now because you've made me think about it, thanks for asking. They, and their questions, were a constant reminder, and a constant irritation, of what I was missing. I preferred the company of strangers who had no knowledge and even less interest in my past. The contact was momentary: all we cared about was achieving orgasm. The fleeting physical intimacy was one step up from masturbation.

The young man said his name was John, but he was obviously lying. I told him truthfully my name was Richard. On the few occasions I used his name he looked at me as if he had no idea to whom I was referring. After that, I skipped using his pseudonym. He was going to be just another short-lived substitute for Jake; one that I could hug and kiss for warmth and that gooey feeling that comes with holding another human being close.

He said he was in town for a weekend conference. From where he came I had no idea. He was skimpy on detail and I was not about to question him as he became skittish if my curiosity got the better of me. He obviously had something to hide, although he was not wearing a wedding ring. I guessed he was so far in the back of the closet he was in Narnia. Perhaps he escaped to the city from wherever he came on a regular basis to quench his gay desire. I didn't mind being one in a line of however many or few.

His conference, however, seemed the farthest thing from his mind when we awoke on Saturday morning. He was the first man who had stayed the night. Normally, they blew a load (or two) and left. John stayed. In fact, John stayed the entire weekend. We never left the house. I made breakfast and dinner when we felt peckish, but most of the time we screwed: in the bedroom, in the living room, in the kitchen, in the bathroom – in fact, the only room I think we missed was the garage and that only because there was no room to maneuver around my SUV.

I'd never felt as comfortable around another man as I did around John. Except around Jake.

John was like a puppy, so eager and grateful for scraps of affection I was more than happy to feed him. I'd had no one to share them with for months and I was afraid I was going to become so overbearing, John would flee. No, he lapped it up as if his life was in the midst of an affection drought. I so wanted to ask but I wasn't prepared to do anything to jeopardize the weekend. He got up for breakfast that Saturday, showered, and dressed as if to head off for whatever it was his conference was discussing – another secret he kept; it could have been anything from nuclear disarmament through to crochet patterns for seniors.

"Scrambled eggs on toast with a side order of grilled tomato and sausage?" I asked, disappointed when he wandered in fully clothed. I was still in my briefs and dressing gown, hoping we'd have time for another quick fumble before he left.

6

"Yeah, thanks," he said.

He looked embarrassed in the bright light of day. "Um…" he began.

"It's okay," I interrupted. "As much as I loved your company, and the fact you're great sex, and we seemed to hit it off, I'm not going to ask your phone number because I know it will be fake, just like your name is almost certainly not John."

He blushed, revealing the truth of my statement.

I smiled. "Don't sweat it. If you're ever in town and would like to hook up for a couple of drinks, a chat, or…whatever, you know where I live. I can guarantee I won't be sitting by the window like some star-struck teenager cursing that you never show up. Too old for all that."

He must have been holding his breath because he suddenly sighed. "Thanks."

"You've had other men get a bit clingy in the past?"

He nodded his head. "Yeah. Like super glue."

"Goes with the territory when you're as good-looking as God."

He laughed. "You think so."

I continued to keep an eye on the sizzling breakfast, as I counted off his good points. "Good looking? Tick. Hot body? Tick. Fantastic kisser? Tick.

Dick of death? Tick. An ass to make the angels weep? Tick. Incredible personality? Tick."

"You're just saying that because you want to fuck me," he said.

"Been there, done that," I joked.

"And very well, I might add. Speaking of hot ass, yours is not to be sneezed at either."

"Unless I put pepper in my butthole."

"Ouch."

This awkwardness was why a lot of guys avoid the 'morning after.' Too weird unless it's the mutually agreed beginning of something stronger. I knew this wasn't going in that direction. Sure, we had a rapport but it was a one-time only. He had his secrets that he was not about to share with me.

We ate our breakfast in silence although I caught him staring at me on a number of occasions. Finally, he pushed his plate aside, and asked, "Why doesn't a handsome dude like you have a wife or a boyfriend?"

"I did, but he died. We were together for fifteen years." I left it at that. If he was interested, he would ask for more details. After thinking it over for a while, he did. Twenty minutes later, John had the potted history of my relationship. It felt so good to discuss it with someone neither of us had known. It was cathartic, although I did seem to feel Jake slipping from my mind like sand through my fingers at the beach.

"That is so cool," he said. "Not the part where he dies of course but that you guys had that special love for so long."

"You've never been in love?" I asked.

He hesitated, although it was written all over his face that he wanted to share. "I've never told anyone this before. I was in love once, but it didn't work out."

"Oh?"

That was all the encouragement he needed to continue. "The love of my life."

"So far," I added.

"Yeah, well, I think your first is the strongest. Or, at least the one you remember most."

I nodded agreement.

"The…uh…other person was…an athlete."

He fumbled over the pronouns, getting hopelessly jumbled. It was becoming difficult to follow the story. I held my hand up to get him to stop.

"Okay, let's just for the sake of argument dispense with all the prevarication. Let's just say your love was another dude-" He went to object. "It's only pretend. It doesn't make you gay or anything. Let's just pretend for the sake of clarity in your story. Okay? What will we call him?"

He seemed relieved. "How about…" He pretended to think it over but the name was obviously on the tip of his tongue, "Finn? He was a football jock. Like me. He was my best friend. We went through high school together and on to college. We had big plans about leaving our home town and heading to a big city to pursue our dreams of success and wealth. I was stupid, I guess. I saw us living together, not like husband and wife or anything faggy." He shrugged. "I guess I was naïve. I thought we could live together as good buddies. When we were growing up we sort of experimented… you know…sexually. A hand job or jerking off together while we watched porn. I even dared to give him a blow job one night when we were both drunk. After that, he pretended to be drunk a lot. He never reciprocated. It wasn't until we were in college that our whole relationship changed. No more jerking off together, no more blow jobs. He had a string of girlfriends. I didn't mind too much because I could hear him banging away because our bedroom walls were so thin. I'd listen as he fucked the girls, and I'd unload my balls. The chicks were always gone by the morning.

"Until he met Cilla. She not only stayed for breakfast, she as good as moved in within a couple of weeks, and became a permanent fixture within months. I didn't like it. I didn't like the way she monopolized

Finn's time. I didn't like the way she fawned over him while we watched TV together. I didn't like the way…I didn't like anything about her. I tried turning Finn against her but it didn't work. I tried to sabotage the relationship but it always went wrong and just drove Finn into her corner against me. We didn't go out together anymore and even the invitations to go out as a threesome dried up. I'd been sidelined. One day after I suppose I'd tried one last time to drive a wedge between them, the look of disgust at my treachery was obvious on Finn's face, Cilla came to me and accused me of being a petty jealous fag. 'Finn can't stand to look at your weepy fag face any more. We both want you gone,' she said. I stood up to her and told her I didn't want to leave. 'In that case, I may have to have a word to your parents about what you used to like doing to Finn.' I was shocked. I didn't think he would ever tell anyone. 'Listen fag, you want your reputation trashed?' She knew she was holding all the aces; my family was important in the town and having it revealed their son had sucked cock would have devastated them as well as affected their status. I moved out a week later, taking with me the knowledge that I was in love with Finn."

I sympathized. "That must have hurt."

His eyes were glistening, so I held him in my arms. "What happened to them?"

His voice was muffled in my dressing gown but I made out, "They eventually got married. Finn put all his dreams on hold and now he's got a mediocre job with a mediocre company in a mediocre town. They have three kids that he idolizes. He works his ass off to support them and she plays up behind his back. I tried telling him once but all I got for my trouble was a bloody nose. I don't see him anymore."

"Still, he's lodged in there." I tapped John's chest near his heart.

John sighed, wiped his eyes and stepped out my embrace. "I've never told anyone that before."

"Feel better?"

"It's amazing. Like a heavy weight has been lifted off me."

"Come on, finish your coffee and I'll drive you to your conference."

"You don't have to do that."

"No, but it's the least I can do after the spectacular time you gave me last night."

His face went red. "Um...what have you got planned for the weekend?"

"Nothing much. A bit of washing, a bit of lazing by the pool, catching up on reading. That's about all."

He took a deep breath. "Want some company?"

"What about your conference?"

"Fuck that, you're a lot more interesting than a boring old conference."

I suspected the talkfest was a ruse to not only get away from his home town and whatever awaited him there but also to get away from his one-night stand in case it turned out less than successful.

"I'd love you to stay. "

So, stay he did, and in the remainder of the weekend he did more to reawaken me to the possibilities that life still held than anything I'd done in the past five months. John was tender, John was smart, and John fucked like a bunny rabbit running on supercharged batteries. If he hadn't left Monday morning, after postponing his Sunday night departure, I think I would have died of over stimulation. I couldn't believe my balls could manufacture that much cum or that my sphincter didn't snap from excessive use. I think every organ and orifice got a thorough working over. On both of us.

We both knew it was a one-off and that we'd never see each other again which made it bitter-sweet but still more meaningful than all the other recent one-night relationships combined. I hadn't felt this giddy and girlish since Jake. I knew I should say something in an attempt to keep John with me but he had a life unknown to me back in his unmentioned home town.

I dropped him at the airport and I suppose I could have followed him to spy on the flight he took but to what purpose? In the end, I plucked up the courage to say, "I wish you could stay." He appeared genuinely crestfallen when he replied, "I wish I didn't have other commitments."

As we wrestled his suitcase out of the boot of the car – we'd picked it up from his unused hotel room on the way – I thanked him. "It's been one of the most wonderful weekends since Jake died. Thanks for bringing me out of my shell. I was beginning to suffocate in there. You've given me a new lease of life."

"You've given me more than you know. A new awareness of myself. I've had to own up to a few truths that I didn't want to admit to myself before. I don't think, though, that I have the courage to make the necessary changes." Self-awareness only seemed to have made him sad.

I gave the only advice I was qualified to give. "You only have one life."

As he walked to the check-in counter he looked determined but didn't glance back even as he headed for his departure gate. I waited a while longer before I headed back home. He'd left behind a huge gap in my life even though I'd known him a little less than seventy-two hours. There was a certain wistfulness to the occasion but I noticed my step was lighter and I was actually whistling, a broad smile lighting up my face as I headed back to the car park.

My good mood changed a few days later when my one and only attempt at heterosexual intercourse rang. I was surprised she had the number. We'd never kept in touch once I left town because Melinda had found some bunny to marry her and bring my daughter up as his own. I wasn't even privy to whether he knew it wasn't his; all I knew was I was off the hook for paying child maintenance at a time that I was first starting out. Extra debt would have crippled me and it would have taken years more, if not decades, to get to the financially comfortable position in which I now found myself.

I didn't recognize the number that came up on my phone, or the voice as it asked, "Is that Richard Bentley?"

"Yes, it is," I replied perkily.

I was so out of contact with that part of my past, that when she said, "This is Melinda," I said "Melinda who?" before my brain could engage.

Her voice was icy. "Melinda, the mother of your daughter. How many Melinda's do you know?"

I wasn't going to buy into an argument, especially with a woman I hadn't seen in twenty years. "What can I do for you, Melinda?"

"Well, that's pretty direct," she huffed.

"What do you want?"

"I don't want anything," she replied.

There had to be more to it. I waited.

"Your daughter wants something."

"What?"

I heard the deep inhale of breath as if she really didn't want to have this conversation. "She wants you to come to her wedding."

"Why?"

"She...um...wants to meet her real dad."

"What about Bruce...Brian...Bob...Barry... Boris..."

She let me flounder for a moment before she said, "Craig."

"Is that his name?"

"Was his name."

"You're divorced?"

"Widowed."

Well, we had that in common. I suppose I could have been a little more empathetic but it's difficult to care about someone you only knew at school and who took advantage of you and who you hadn't had anything to do with in two decades. I made a few coughs and grunts which she took for condolences and said, "Thanks." I wasn't about to share my private life with her. It wasn't a game of one-upmanship. "Did you receive the invitation?"

"Yeah, it's here somewhere."

"It's important, Ricky."

I shuddered. No one, but no one, called me Ricky any more. I was Richard or, if I knew you really well, you could call me Rich. Never Ricky.

"When is it?"

She gave me the date which was five weeks away. Quickly consulting my diary I discovered I had a few appointments around that period but they'd be easily shuffled. "I'll see what I can do."

"She wants you to give her away."

Oh, shit.

"I don't do all this wedding shit, Melinda. And it's not like I've had anything to do with Marcie, apart from her conception and I'm not even sure my mind was on the job when I did that."

It was a cheap jab but the way Melinda had taken advantage of me still rankled.

"It's about Marcie, not you or me," she said.

"Okay, I can change a few appointments but I'll be leaving straight after the wedding reception."

"Do what you have to? You can stay here at the house if you want."

"Thanks for offer but I'd rather a hotel."

"Suit yourself."

"What do the couple-to-be want for a gift?"

"A Maserati would be nice but failing that, they have one of those internet thingies with a list." She gave me the log-in and I wrote it on a scrap of paper. Sure, I could afford a Maserati but that was not something I'd be buying an estranged daughter and her prospective husband.

"Who's the lucky man?" I hoped I kept the sarcasm out of my voice.

"A real catch. Important family. Colin Featherstone. A financial wiz. Great prospects. Enough money to keep Marcie in a manner that she wants. Oh, and he's good-looking."

I had yet to hear the word 'love' enter the conversation. "Can I…"

"I'd really rather you didn't bring your boyfriend or twinkie or whatever you people call your fuck of the day."

That was so unexpected; I was momentarily lost for words. When I did respond my voice was a low growl. "I was going to ask if you needed some help financially with the wedding. It may also be of interest to you that I won't be bringing my boyfriend because he died five months ago after we had fifteen wonderful years together."

I didn't expect sympathy but all I got was "Whatever."

"There is one thing, however, I do insist upon before I even contemplate coming to the wedding and that is I will not pretend to be something I'm not. I am an out gay man and that is exactly how I will present myself."

"As long as you leave the catering staff alone."

Was she trying to provoke me?

"Precisely how many people know that I'm gay, Melinda?"

"Uh…only me."

"Then I suggest for you had better fill our daughter in quick smart to see if she wants her faggy old man to turn up. Get Marcie to ring me to confirm, otherwise I won't be there. Understood?"

"Understood. I can't pretend I want you here for such an important event, but, as I said, this is for my daughter."

It was two days later that Marcie called. "Oh, daddy, I may call you that may'nt I?"

What twenty-year-old spoke like that?

"I'd prefer you called me Richard."

"Um…okay. Mum told me your news. That's too bad, but I still want you here."

"What's too bad, Marcie?"

"That you'll have a miserable life and die a lonely old man."

"Why would I do that?"

"Because you're a fa…because you're homosexual."

"Who put such ridiculous ideas in your head?"

"The Reverend Featherstone, Colin's dad. He says that the homosexual agenda will lead to the destruction of the civilized world as we know it. Do you know that some of them even want to get married? Can you believe the nerve of some people?"

Marcie kept up the homophobic claptrap in the same enthusiastic voice she had for her wedding. She sounded like a total bubble-headed bimbo. I wondered how my sperm could have produced this airhead. I let her prattle on for a little while longer before I sought her assurance that me and my homosexual agenda would be welcome at the wedding.

"Of course, Richard. As long as you don't try to convert anyone, especially not Colin."

I doubted I'd be even remotely interested in any man that found Marcie and her attitudes palatable. I, on the other hand, could grit my teeth and put up with it. Before Marcie hung up, she added, "Please, don't wear a dress or anything like that. That would be sooo embarrassing."

I knew now there was no likelihood of any close connection between the two of us so, as soon as she was gone, I arranged to have coffee with Flax, my best mate. I needed to talk. After I'd explained the situation and he'd run through his lecture of gay self-respect, he stopped his gay banter and looked at me knowingly. "Okay, what's the real problem here, Rich?"

"What do you mean?" I asked.

"Don't give me that wide-eyed innocent look. I know you better than you know yourself."

We had history. He'd always been a good friend to Jake and me and after Jake's death he'd thought the best way to cheer me up was to fuck me. I could have turned him down but I needed the warmth of another body in my bed and in Flax's case, what a body! He was a personal trainer in the gayest gym in town and popular as fuck which he did on an almost monotonously regular basis. He was so hot I sometimes thought the sun would be envious. He had even been known to seduce the most hetero of men who patronized his establishment.

It was no use prevaricating, he'd worm it out of me anyway.

"I guess I'm feeling my age."

Flax looked to the heavens, rolling his eyes in disgust. "That must make me Methuselah then, I'm three years older than you."

"You don't look it," I complained.

"It's how you feel that matters. It's your attitude to life. And, Rich, if I may so–" I put my hand up to stop him but he simply ignored it. "I'm not asking your permission, mate, I'm telling you."

I sighed to signal my surrender.

"You're only as old as you feel."

I mouthed the words along with him.

"Then, I feel ancient," I added.

"Go and get yourself laid." That was Flax's solution to all the shit life could throw at a person.

"That's part of the problem."

"What? A good-looking dude like you can't get laid? Bullshit."

I cringed under the onslaught. "Give me a chance to explain."

"Oh oh, this must be serious then." He did that thing about locking his lips and smiled at me to go on.

"It's a combination of things. The marriage of my daughter…"

He interrupted. "I thought you didn't even like her."

"And I thought you were going to be quiet."

He keyed his lips again but I knew it was the sort of lock that didn't guarantee any sort of safety from his prying, or his superiority because of his supposedly better life skills. He signaled that I should continue.

Giving me his undivided attention was almost as off-putting as his constant interruptions.

"Marcie's wedding has merely been the catalyst reminding me of what my life is missing since Jake died."

Flax's solutions were always simple. "Go out and find another Jake then." When I didn't respond as I would usually he searched my face.

"Oh. My. God. You've met someone haven't you?"

"Yes and no. That's the other part of it. The wedding was the final straw. A couple of weeks back I found a man and we had a real connection…"

I told him the whole story about my weekend with John; not that there was a lot of story to tell.

"Don't you see, Rich," Flax was using his 'kind' voice, "If you can find that sort of connection with a total stranger then you can find it anywhere. It's just a matter of looking."

"I guess so."

"I know so."

I spent the next five minutes babbling about John and his good points until Flax put up his hand. "Enough already. Go get him if he means that much to you."

"I don't know anything about him I admitted. I really didn't think I'd get it this bad."

"No phone number?"

"No, and he was obviously using a fake name."

"Rich, you really need to get yourself back in the swing of life. If you like a man the first thing you do is look in his wallet while he's in the shower. A driver's license will tell you everything you need to know."

I must have looked horrified at the invasion of privacy.

"Don't go all goggle-eyed on me, Rich. How do you think I know which men are worthy of a second or maybe even a third meeting? All the info you need is right there in their wallet."

My response was sarcasm. "Excuse me for having more respect for my partners. Also, I didn't know a license came with the word 'compatible' stamped across it these days."

"You don't get it, do you? You get his license you get his details. Facebook and Google are your friends. Consult them regularly. Otherwise you may miss that he tortures puppies and is married with five wives and sixteen kids."

I had to laugh. If only life were as open as Flax found it. To me, modern dating was as fraught as the forest in which Hansel and Gretel found themselves, a candy-covered cottage of treats disguising a trap. I didn't want to get burned.

"You really going to this wedding?"

I shrugged. "I guess. I've never seen my grown-up daughter, plus I haven't been back to the town since I left twenty years ago."

"Who was that guy you used to talk about all the time? You were at high school together."

"Vince?"

"That's the one. You couldn't stop talking about him when we first met. You were always going to go back home and confront him, tell him you're gay and see what he had to offer."

"Then I met Jake."

"Well, if you get bored in Breederville, you can always look up old Vince."

"Or some of the other jocks I used to play football with."

Suddenly, the trip didn't seem such a bad idea, after all. There'd been a certain amount of adolescent experimentation with my jock buddies and there were a few studs I'd be more than happy to help take it to the next level. But as my departure date approached, I wondered how difficult it would be to butt my head up against the entrenched homophobia I was expecting. I'd warned both Mel and Marcie during one of their periodic phone calls to update me that I wouldn't stand for any overt hostility. "Covert's okay then, is it?" Melinda asked with vicious glee.

"No sort of hostility is acceptable and, for Marcie's sake, you'd better make that known. I will not hesitate to walk at any stage of the proceedings. Please make that abundantly clear to this Colin character and his family and any of the guests who may think to make a big man of themselves by goading the fag. Got it?"

"Loud and clear," Mel said. "You sure have changed from the wimpy little guy I had to get drunk to fuck me."

"If only you knew," I replied before disconnecting.

I might have had Melinda's word for it but that didn't necessarily hold true for everyone else who was going to be at the wedding. I was incredibly nervous as my flight landed at Breederville regional airport. Melinda told me that there'd be a welcoming committee and although I didn't expect a brass band or the Westboro Baptist Church with placards proclaiming 'God hates fags' I also wasn't quite prepared for the hot young man holding a placard that read, 'Welcome, Ricky Flanagan.' As I made my way over to the mountain of muscle barely contained in his tight-fitting casual clothes, I realized why Mel and Marcie might tell me to keep my hands off the prospective groom. My daughter had great taste in men.

He smiled as he noticed me wending my way through the crowds toward him. He grabbed my suitcase although I was reluctant to let it go. "I'm still young enough to carry my own bag," I retorted.

"I was just being polite," he said.

"I know," I admitted. "I'm just a bit wound up at the moment. It's strange returning after twenty years."

"You think you're wound up? Everyone here is walking on egg shells."

I liked the big lug already.

"The car's in the parking lot. What hotel are you staying at?"

He whistled when I told him. "Fancy."

If there's one rule I abide by it's that if you're going to return to your home town, high school or old job then make sure you're incredibly successful in your field of endeavor first and then make sure you rub your old friends' and enemies' noses in it. No point otherwise.

As he loaded my suitcase into the boot of the car, he said, "You're a bit of a mystery man, Mr. Flanagan. Nobody here seems to know what happened to you after you left twenty years ago. Especially after your parents moved away."

"This town hasn't caught up with Google then? I assume you do have internet connection?" I was being a twat and I knew it.

The young man gave me a serve of my own medicine. "I guess no one really cared once the fag left town."

"Ouch," I responded. "I guess I deserve that. What's say we start again? I held my hand out. I'm Richard Flanagan, father of the bride."

The young man rubbed his hand down the leg of his trousers before offering it to me. His grip was firm but not crushingly so. "Pleased to meet you, Mr. Flanagan, I'm Troy Marshall, the groom's best mate."

"I thought you were the groom."

Troy laughed. "Nah. I wish."

The conversation continued once we were in the car. Troy looked at me as if to weigh up how much he should say. "You're not at all like I expected, Mr. Flanagan. You look like a jock."

"I was a jock, Troy. A few years ago now, but I looked almost as good as you twenty years ago."

"Wow."

"Please call me…oh, what the fuck, call me Ricky."

"Thanks, man. It's so hard trying to remember the Mr. Flanagan shit. Oh, sorry."

"What for?"

"I swore."

"Holy fuckin' mother of god," I laughed. "You'll go to hell, no doubt about it."

Troy looked over at me sheepishly to see if I was serious. I guess my grin gave it away. Troy relaxed.

"You really a fag?" Troy asked.

"Why? Are you interested?"

After Troy got control of the wheel after almost running us off the road, he asked, "Are you?"

Was this a test of some sort? "Troy, you are an amazing looking guy and what I've seen of your personality so far, you'd be a real catch for some lucky girl...or guy."

"That's really nice of you to say, Mr....Ricky. Nah, I dig girls. Especially one little honey."

He looked so despondent, I took a chance and guessed. "Marcie?"

"Yeah. But she'll do so much better with Colin. He's smart, he's intelligent, he's got prospects. He's got looks."

"He must be quite something if he's better looking than you." I was serious.

"You hitting on me, Mr. Flanagan?" Troy didn't seem perturbed by the idea.

"Maybe if I was twenty years younger," I admitted.

Troy appraised me. "Maybe if I was gay..."

I laughed.

"What do you do, Troy?"

"I work in a second-hand car yard."

"You like the job?"

"It sucks. But I ain't got the smarts to do what I really want."

"Which is?"

"I want to set up my own gym."

"The town doesn't have one already?"

"Yeah, but it's so impersonal. Big building, glass and chrome shit. Costs a deltoid and a bicep just to get in the door."

"Not your sort of place?"

"I want to work with people who don't eat proper. You know obesity is the number one killer in this country? My mum was what doctors call clinically obese. She wanted to lose the weight but we couldn't afford the fees at the gym and she didn't have the willpower to do it on her own. Plus she needed advice on what to eat and lots of support but there was none. Killed her in the end."

"I'm sorry," I muttered. "Obviously your gym would be different to the norm."

"Yeah, it would welcome people who were overweight, too frightened to look in the mirror in case they saw themselves. I want to help people. Like that Richard Simmons guy."

I twigged. "That's what everyone is expecting me to be like, isn't it?" They thought I was going to be a screamer.

Troy appeared embarrassed. "Yep."

"Sorry to disappoint you."

"Hey, I'm not disappointed," Troy said enthusiastically. "I think you're okay. If anyone gives you any trouble you just refer them to me."

"Thanks, Troy. And for what it's worth, I wish you were marrying my daughter."

He looked sheepish. "Me, too." Then he brightened up. "Hey, you want I should drive you past the perfect spot for my gym. It's all just a dream but if you don't got one then you don't have nothing to strive for, right?" I nodded agreement. "I couldn't get through my day without something to keep me going. I worked out it will only take me seventy-seven years on my current pay packet to save up enough for a deposit." That fact didn't seem to get him down.

"I'd love to hear more about your gym, Troy." It never hurt to spend time with a hot man. All I was doing, of course, was delaying the inevitable. We drove past the old building that was up for sale while Troy sketched in his vision, bringing it vividly to life, although a pervasive sense of sadness colored his speech.

"You've really thought this gym idea of yours through?"

He looked sheepish. "Not much to do is a used car sale yard in between prospective buyers. I juggle the figures to see if I can make it work better."

When we got to my hotel, I checked in while Troy waited. He'd been instructed to take me straight to meet my daughter. I suspected even the short detour was a capital offense.

"Why don't you come up to my room and wait while I get changed?" I expected suspicion on Troy's part but I think he was just happy that someone listened to his dreams for a change.

In the elevator taking us the twelfth floor, I asked, "What makes you think you can make your idea work? What experience have you had?"

"Gee, Mr. Flanagan, can anyone guarantee that their idea will work? But I volunteer as a sort of personal trainer at the aged care facility here in town. Three times a week, I work with a physiotherapist and she seems to think what I do makes a difference. You gotta keep your body active as well as your brain, I know that for sure, even if it's just rotating your arms while you're in a chair."

"Troy, did you look me up on the net?"

"I tried, but there was no Ricky Flanagan that fitted what I was told about you."

"What about the others?"

"Nah. Marcie said she'd rather not know in case you turned out to be fat and gross. Colin's nervous as a grasshopper with fleas and seems ready to bolt. No one else cares."

"Okay. You mind if I come and watch you at the aged care home some time before I leave?"

"Really? Gosh, that would make my day. Everybody thinks I'm wasting my time. I thought you were just being nice asking me all about it. I run off at the mouth if anyone shows the tiniest bit of interest."

"You got calculations on paper or computer?"

"Both."

"Mind if I take a look at them. I might be able to give you some advice. Might be able to help you achieve your dream by the time you reach, say, sixty-eight."

"You're funny, Mr. Flanagan."

"Seriously, Troy."

"Sure, I got figures but I've been over them and over them and they add up. No way would I cut corners."

I headed toward the bedroom. "Give me fifteen, then we you can take me to meet my daughter."

I closed the door while I had a quick shower in the en suite bathroom. I must admit, I dressed to impress, so much so that Troy gave me a whistle of admiration when I emerged.

"I hope I look as good as you do when I'm your age Mr. F."

I took it as a compliment.

Back in the car my stomach had butterflies; I was mere minutes away from meeting a daughter I had only ever seen as a baby. Now that I needed Troy to babble on about his gym to keep my mind otherwise distracted, he sat at the wheel mute.

"Something wrong?" I enquired.

He sighed. "I guess I was always hoping Marcie would see that Colin is not right for her and she'd finally look at me."

"Not gonna happen?"

"No."

"What will you do?"

He shrugged. "Wait around a few years to make sure the marriage sticks then move on if it does. I hope they're happy, I really do. But at the same time…"

I squeezed his arm, feeling the incredible muscle beneath his shirt sleeve. "I understand."

"I don't," he admitted.

"You've got it bad."

We spent the rest of the short trip in silence until Troy beeped his horn as he pulled up outside a house that had so many cars in the driveway there was no room for any more. It was a modest brick home, the lawn neatly trimmed, the garden mainly a collection of local shrubs and bushes that needed minimum care. No one rushed out to greet us; no dog came bounding across the lawn, its tongue hanging out in welcome.

Troy seemed uncomfortable, almost as if he were embarrassed for me.

"Don't sweat it, mate," I said. "I'm not exactly expecting a hero's welcome."

"They're probably out the back and didn't hear me."

"Nice try. At least it tells me what sort of stay I have ahead of me." I was glad I'd chosen a hotel I could escape to when things got too rough. Had I stayed with Melinda, I suspect I wouldn't have lasted the duration. I moaned that I'd chosen to spend four days in this godforsaken hole.

The front door was open in expectation of my arrival. I don't know why small-town folk think the ability to leave their door unlocked is a sign of a civilized community and then express surprise when they're robbed or a loved one is murdered in their bed. Give me the paranoia of a big city. There I'll sleep secure.

Troy called out as he opened the screen door to usher me inside. Maybe it was a signal to put away their shotguns, that we were friend not foe, although my status was probably very much undecided at the moment. We found them in the kitchen. No wonder nobody heard the car horn as Marcie, I assume it was my daughter as she had on a bridal veil, was caterwauling fit to wake the dead. "I told that fuckin' girl in the bridal shop I wanted beige not white. 'Do I look like a fuckin' virgin to you?' I told her.' Jesus."

There was a lot more in this vein as Troy and I stood in the doorway watching the drama unfold, not daring to interrupt. There were two other women in the kitchen, both of them ignoring Marcie's outburst, expecting her to run out of steam eventually. I recognized Mel who seemed impatient for the stream of abuse to settle down. When it didn't look like the end was in sight any time soon, Mel snapped, "For Christ's sake Marcie, you're doing my head in and I don't need a migraine on the day your fag dad is coming to pay a visit. Now, hush up, it is fucking beige, not white."

Did anyone ever get a fonder welcome?

Troy cleared his throat loudly and all three women turned as one. The years had not been kind to Melinda. She was brassy and dumpy, probably a popular combination in a widow. She wouldn't want for male attention. The dark roots were beginning to show in her dirty blonde hair, her face lined and her eyes baggy: a woman old beyond her years. Our daughter was apparently a handful. She also had a mouth on her like a trashcan.

While Mel looked daggers at me, the two unfamiliar women gave me the once over, and Marcie shrieked with manufactured delight. "Daddy," she screamed, crossing the room briskly to fling her arms around me and plant a wet sloppy kiss on my cheek. "What color do you call this?" she asked thrusting the offending veil into my hands. I had to make a split second decision. Nothing was ever going to get Melinda onside, even if I agreed with her definition of the color. On the other hand, my stay might be made more comfortable if I sided with the ear-piercing brattiness of our daughter. Simple choice. "It's white," I agreed.

Marcie turned triumphantly to the women in the room. "See, I told you it was white."

It was beige.

Melinda upped her death ray eyes a notch or two attempting to nuke me on the spot.

"Hello, Mel."

"Ricky." Melinda had no time for me and obviously no intention of putting herself out. "Meet Cora Featherstone, Colin's mum."

I smiled at the prim and prune-faced old cow standing at the sink. "Pleased to meet you."

Her response was a grunt that left no doubt she'd been prepped to dislike me from the start.

I suppose the uncomfortable feeling in the room might have dissipated eventually but Marcie screamed in a voice that could probably be heard suburbs away, "Colin, get your ass in here. My dad has arrived."

I glanced at Troy who had the appearance of a lovesick idiot as he pined for Marcie. Love, in this case, was definitely deaf as well as blind. I didn't have time to wonder too much about the vagaries of the heart as Colin Featherstone, the man who was about to marry this harridan posing as my offspring, entered, wiping the perspiration from his face with a bandana. He must have been working on his car as his hands and face were streaked in places with grease and dirt. He looked up and we both gasped loudly. He stuttered, "Richard?" as I said, "John?" at the same time.

Marcie looked between the two of us quizzically. "Have you two met?" she asked.

I hesitated, leaving it to Colin/John to answer. I'd take my lead from him.

"No, I was just surprised he'd arrived already," Colin said, excusing his behavior.

"He was due an hour ago," Melinda groused.

"I bet Troy was showing daddy that dreadful old building that he dreams of turning into a home for fatties."

The women all laughed uproariously. I failed to see the joke.

"Why did you call him John?" Marcie asked.

I'd had an opportunity to fabricate a story while they picked on Troy. "Marcie, your Colin is the spitting image of a friend I have back in the city whose name is John. The likeness is uncanny."

They were either not of a curious bent or my explanation was sufficient because the subject was dropped immediately. Colin pleaded with his eyes to let the matter drop.

"Working on your car, mate?" I asked in order to break the ice.

"Just making sure everything is tuned up for the honeymoon."

Mel suggested that I go and help him.

I got the impression the women wanted me gone so they could talk about me and grill Troy for any pertinent dirt. The atmosphere in the house was poisonous. Colin stuttered, backing away from me as if I'd been sent as a hit man. "Uh uh..." His mouth kept opening and closing like a goldfish but he seemed unable to string two coherent words together let alone make any sort of a statement. I gave him a gentle shove.

Once outside the house, the babble inside increased to such a level that what they were saying was hardly a secret.

"OMG!" Marcie screamed. And, yes, she said the letters not the words. "Did you get a load of my dad? He's gorgeous. I hope I got his genes."

"She got her mother's personality, though, I'm afraid," I whispered as I grabbed Colin by the arm and steered him toward more privacy in the garage.

"What the fuck are you doing here?" Colin hissed.

I smiled sweetly. "I thought that was obvious. I'm the sperm donor, otherwise known as dad."

"Why have you turned up now?"

"D'uh, because I was invited. Pressure was brought to bear by her harridan of a mother that I was required to do my duty by our daughter."

"I thought you were gay?"

"Marcie is as the result of a very determined girl at a prom who had designs on one very eligible but very closeted gay college jock who she got drunk enough to do the deed. That a satisfactory explanation?"

"You can't stay for the wedding."

"That's fine by me. This is a disaster waiting to happen. I'll just go inside and tell Marcie that her dad can't stay for her nuptials because he accidentally fucked her future husband. Not once, not twice, but repeatedly over what was one of the most wonderful weekends of his life."

Colin freaked.

"For fuck's sake, Colin. I was joking. I'm not going to out you."

"I'm not gay," he said tersely.

"If you marry Marcie you soon will be."

"What's that supposed to mean?"

"Get a grip, Colin. It was another joke. Where's your sense of humor fled to?"

He was having difficulty breathing.

"Slow breaths, Colin. In. Out. In. Out. Put your head down."

When he regained his composure, I put my hand up to stop him speaking. "Hear me out. I can't very well just up and leave without a very good reason. Now we can play this a number of ways. You can punch me and call me a faggot in front of your future in-laws and I'll leave humiliated and ashamed that I attempted to proposition you. Or, we can be very adult about the situation and pretend that you and I did not share a weekend of fabulous sex a month or so ago. I'm sure my skills as an actor are up to that subterfuge. What about yours?"

Colin was spiteful. "I wish I'd never met you."

"The feeling is quite mutual," I replied. "Of course, had you told the truth and given your real name, and the fact you were in the city to sow your gay wild oats before marrying, I would have known where I stood.

As it was, you left me with such wonderful memories I haven't been able to get you out of my mind."

"You haven't?"

"Do you know how often people make a connection like we did? It's about as rare as finding a novel these days that doesn't contain a vampire. If I never saw you again my memories would have faded with time but seeing you here today, all it's done is reignited my passion." To emphasize the point I placed Colin's hand on the front of my trousers over my very prominent bulge. I'd gone rock hard the moment I set eyes on him. He groaned without removing his hand. I dared to rub my hand over his crotch to find him similarly stimulated.

"Seems we both have a problem here, Colin. What are we going to do about it?"

His reply was immediate, although definitely non-verbal. He dropped to his knees and grabbed for the fly of my trousers, unzipping me so fast I feared for the skin on my cock if it got caught in the teeth. He plunged his hand into the opening and had my cock extracted from my briefs in seconds, shoving his mouth over the knob and half the shaft before I'd had a chance to catch my breath. He sucked like a man dying of thirst.

His marriage was in deep shit.

"Colin, mate," I said, attempting to get him up off his knees. "Not here. Come back to my hotel. It'll be private there."

He nodded and stood up, helping me put my cock away. "I have an idea. You wait here while I set the scene." He was shaking so badly I didn't think it was a good idea for him to be seen in such a state. I raced back into the house. As soon as I entered the room, conversation stopped. "Look…um…Colin needs a part for his car and I'm gonna drive him into town to pick it up. It'll give me a chance to bond better with our little girl's future husband."

Melinda was vicious. "Bond? Is that what you faggots call it these days?"

"Mum," Marcie warned. "I think that's a great idea. Make sure you don't shock him too much, daddy, he's very shy."

"Don't be late, we're having dinner with Cora and the Reverend Featherstone tonight at six," Melinda added.

"What? I was hoping to catch up on my sleep. I was up at sparrow's fart this morning to catch the plane."

"Language," admonished Cora Featherstone.

"Oh, blow it out your ass," I said sweetly. "I heard Marcie curse until even God got embarrassed earlier but I didn't hear a peep out of you then."

She clutched her bosom indignantly.

"Can I borrow your keys, Troy?"

He retrieved them from his pocket and tossed them over to me, the beginnings of a smile quivering around the edge of his lips. "We'll be back in time for dinner," I said as I slammed out the back door.

The indignation level rose several notches if my hearing was anything to go by. I nodded to Colin who was still hiding in the garage and we walked down the side of the house to Troy's car. I couldn't be away from this place soon enough. Once we turned out of the street, Colin gave a quick look through the rear window, and relaxed.

"Feeling better now?" I asked.

"It's doing my head in," he said forlornly. "The constant noise, the shouting and arguments. Is that what married life is all about?"

"Don't ask me, I was in a happy non-shouting gay relationship for fifteen years. The heterosexual lifestyle is a mystery to me."

"It's like I'm in a trance," he groaned. "I see this cliff ahead of me but I have to keep walking toward it even though I know it will be the end of me."

"You don't have to go through with it you know."

He was miserable. "If I pulled out now it would kill Marcie, probably lead to estrangement from my family. I'd have to leave town."

I interrupted. "When are you going to get to the bad points?"

"Marcie would be humiliated."

"I think she's pretty resilient. And I'm sure Troy would help her get over any heartache."

"He's a much better mate for her than I will ever be."

"Why don't you chuck it all in?"

"Did you mean what you said earlier?"

"About it being the best weekend and all that?"

"Yeah."

"I haven't been able to forget you."

"Me either."

I'm not sure if Colin was weighing up options as fiercely as I was for the remainder of the journey, and in the hotel elevator, but he had a look of determination on his face. Once inside the room he launched himself at me, clamping his lips over mine, sucking my tongue into his mouth in an oral wrestling match. He hardly gave me a chance to breathe. He was also shucking his clothes as he frantically sought any sort of contact. I pushed him gently toward the bedroom.

The next hour passed all too quickly as we both poured every ounce of passion and longing into our lovemaking. To me it was more than a quick fuck, although time was of the essence. I had weeks of pent-up emotion inside me and if Colin's thirst for sex with me was any indication, he was similarly affected. I was glad I packed condoms and lube, not with any real expectations of running into old friends and college mates, but it's best to be prepared at all times.

Colin was needy in the worst possible way for the future of his marriage. "Fuck me, Richard," he begged, "Fuck me into the floor so I can forget this nightmare I'm in." He lay on his back and stretched his legs in the air. I kneeled down, parting his cheeks, and began to lap at the beautiful cleft in his butt, my nose nudging at his hot hole before exploring it with my tongue. Colin thrashed about on the bed, squirming from side to side as he held my head tight to his ass. As much as I loved getting up close and personal with that cute sphincter of his, what I really wanted was to plunge my cock deep in his bowels so he would never forget me. Reluctantly, I withdrew my tongue. Kneeling, I reached across to the bedside table to extract the condoms and lube from the drawer.

I squeezed the gel on to my fingers and pushed into his tight hole, his muscles gripping me as if they never wanted to let me go. I pushed back and forth, stretching him until he seemed at ease with me inside him. He exhaled a loud sigh of pleasure as he began to push himself back against my hand. "I love that. Oh, God."

I extracted my fingers to line up my lubed cock at his ass entrance and pushed slowly. There was no grunt of pain, no grimace, nothing but the satisfied smile of a man who'd 'come home' to what he really wanted. I caressed his chest, tweaking his nipples briefly, admiring the beautiful man impaled on my gloved cock. I took it easy as I wanted this to last.

Colin looked as if he'd attained a sort of Nirvana, his eyes glazed as he stared up into mine. His cock was hard, his breath raspy and desperate, but I was in this for the long haul. I interspersed a ramming motion between every two or three gentle thrusts just to keep Colin guessing. I hadn't felt this invigorated since my years with Jake. It was both painful and pleasurable remembering my former lover.

"I don't know how many times I've thought of you since I came home," Colin admitted quietly.

I didn't want to spoil the moment but I had to ask, "Why are you getting married then?"

"It's expected of me."

I'd met too many men in my time whose lives had been ruined by expectation, but this was not the occasion in which to attempt to persuade Colin to change his choices. Besides, showing him what he'd be missing was preferable to a lot of anti-erotic jabbering. I let it go to concentrate on giving him pleasure.

I pushed my cock into him at various angles until his grunts revealed the position of his little nub of pleasure. I picked up speed, wrapping my hand around his throbbing prick, milking it in time to my thrusts, little pools of pre-cum oozing out of his slit. "I could fuck you like this forever," I admitted. His satisfied 'Mmm' was all I needed by way of confirmation.

Time was not our friend and I would have preferred a much more leisurely pace but we had to be back for dinner and I knew what sort of tornado of abuse would have been unleashed if we were even ten seconds late.

It was too early to say those magic words which slip off men's lips much too readily so I hoped the look of adoration in my eyes was written large enough that he could see it or at least sense in my behavior that I was developing feelings for him. Okay, that was only going to complicate matters but his marriage was a sham. Even if my feelings didn't result in his returning my affection, if I could simply prevent the mistake that would ruin a number of people's lives, then it was worthwhile, although a little voice in my conscience rankled, "Who appointed you God?"

"I can't hold off much longer," Colin whimpered.

That was the signal for me to increase my pace. I took my hand off his prick to concentrate on fucking his ass. I slammed in and out with more brute force until I had Colin moaning, his hands scrunching the sheets on the bed. I knew he loved dirty talk but it seemed inappropriate right now so I merely expressed my pleasure through grunts and moans. He reciprocated until I gave one almighty shove and my spunk began to fill the latex glove around my cock. Colin's reaction was to gasp, 'Oh, God' over and over as his prick squirted on his chest and stomach, neither of us manipulating him. He'd managed to come just by being fucked.

I remained inside him as I leaned down for his kiss which threatened to keep me hard for much longer. My cock shrank and eventually popped out of his ass as I held the condom in place. Tying the end, I threw it into the trash basket beside the bed, before I lay down next to Colin.

"That was so intense," he said, still attempting to catch his breath.

"Yeah."

As I'd hoped, he was still hard. Like a lot of men he must have found ejaculation without a hand or anything else wrapped around his cock ultimately unsatisfying. "Your turn," I said, handing him a condom.

His eyes widened in surprise. "Really?"

"Fair's fair," I replied, nudging him to move aside. I lay on my back, hoisting my legs in the air holding them close to my chest. Colin scrambled for the lube to grease my entrance. I'm not so much a 50/50 sort of guy as a 70/30. I love to top, just not quite as at home having my ass tapped. No way was I going to deprive Colin of topping me, however, on what might very well turn out to be our last time together. He was so eager it made me wonder if he and Marcie were actually doing it. The image it conjured in my mind threatened to derail my efforts with Colin so I scrubbed my brain to concentrate on our more immediate concerns.

His prepping was more perfunctory than mine had been but it didn't concern me as I was far more experienced. Sure, it burned when he entered my ass much too quickly but I got that under control with a few short deep breaths. I settled back to watch the intense concentration on his face.

"You're so beautiful," I whispered to him.

He responded with a smile and an extra hard thrust into my butt hole.

I relaxed into his rhythm, so comfortable I could have fallen asleep but that's so not a good look when you're trying to impress a man. I heard the catch in Colin's breath so I began to ram my ass back against his cock as he filled me, squeezing my man cunt lips until I had him gasping. He grunted and then shuddered just before he fell on top of me, planting kisses all over my face. I didn't come a second time but then my recuperative powers aren't as formidable as a younger man's.

I let him lie against me for a while, luxuriating in the feel of close personal contact. I already cared about him too much for my own good. The clock beside the bed showed we'd have to get up if we weren't going to arouse suspicion by getting back late for dinner. I slapped Colin's ass affectionately. "Into the shower."

We saved water by washing together although we spent more time fondling each other's cock, as well as kissing and caressing as we rubbed shower gel into those erotic crannies and slick poles until they throbbed again. As much as we both ached to prolong the shower we knew the real world was waiting. I dried his back on the hotel's luxurious towels and he returned the favor. I changed into a different set of casual wear while Colin shrugged on his old work clothes, suggesting we stop by his place on the way back so he, too, could change into something more appropriate.

He was a real chatterbox on the return trip, his inane conversation apparently meant to keep our attention from that clichéd elephant in the room or, in this case, the car. He was still going on as he opened the door to his parents' house, explaining that he wasn't expecting visitors so I might find his bedroom untidy. It wasn't. It was immaculate in its neatness. It was comfortable, if unspectacular, but suited Colin's personality. He offered to make me a coffee but I tapped my watch and he hurried to change in front of me, revealing no embarrassment. It was telling there were no photographs of Marcie anywhere that I could see.

"You don't love Marcie, do you?" I asked gently in order that he wouldn't think it was an accusation.

He had his back to me, pulling on his trousers, when I asked. His head slumped for a moment. "No," he said simply. He tensed as if expecting some sort of lecture but I just reached for him and pulled him onto my lap. I stroked his hair, kissed his eyelids and hugged him. That's all it took. He began to sob, gulping in breath, "What am I going to do?"

I let him cry himself out, holding him to let him know I was there for him. He sniffled and then wiped his nose on the back of his hand. I gave him my handkerchief. "You must think I'm such a coward," he said as he stood up to wipe his eyes.

"I don't know you well enough to make that judgment," I responded truthfully.

My cell phone rang. Glancing at the caller ID, I saw it was Melinda. I slapped Colin on the ass and he went to the bathroom to wash his face.

"Yes, Mel," I said patiently. "We're on our way. We just dropped in to Colin's place so he could change, unless, of course, you wanted him at dinner in his greasy work clothes."

She could hardly complain about that but she tried. I hung up on her.

"Ready?" I asked when Colin emerged, his eyes still red. They'd be better by the time we reached the house.

"I'll never be ready for this," he admitted.

It was a short drive to Melinda's where she made it obvious we'd been gone too long even though we made it back three minutes under the 'curfew.' I was introduced to the Reverend Featherstone who had the same pinched expression as his good wife. He was also cadaverous, as if he had deprived himself of any of life's pleasures including food and drink. His skin was the pallor of vampires and I wondered for a moment whether he had any blood in his veins at all. I went to shake his hand but he skittered it behind his back so I looked the idiot. I lowered my arm and asked politely, "Do you have any relatives in Romania by any chance?"

I'm not sure he understood my meaning, but Colin and Troy snickered.

"We were beginning to worry, daddy," Marcie said as we took our places around the table, hers beside Colin whose arm she clutched proprietorially. "We thought you might have kidnapped him."

"We just got to know each other better," I said.

"How much better is the question," Mel sneered.

Marcie ignored her. "Do you like him, daddy? Isn't he wonderful?"

"That's not the sort of question you ask while I'm at the table, Marcie," Colin said.

"Of course, it is." She was bouncing up and down on her chair with so much excitement it was wearying. "How could he not love you as much as I do?"

"I can assure you, Marcie, without any exaggeration, I already do." I would leave it up the people around the table as to whether I was answering the question about whether I liked Colin or whether I loved him as much as Marcie did. Colin must have picked up on the nuance as he raised an eyebrow.

The meal was delicious, Marcie blabbing indiscreetly that it had been catered because neither she nor her mum were cooks of any note. "Mum burns water," she giggled.

"Colin is a wonderful catch," the Reverend Featherstone said proudly during a pause in Marcie's giggling and squirming.

"This is a match made in heaven," Mel added. "Unlike some others I could mention."

"Now, now," Featherstone reached across the table to pat Mel's arm warmly. "Out of evil some good has arisen. It brought forth Marcie here, one of God's little angels."

Gritting my teeth, I let the insult slide, although Colin almost choked on the soup. "Dad," he said sharply.

"My apologies for telling the truth, Mr. Flanagan. It seems to be that truth telling is out of favor among the younger generation in these modern times."

"Not at all, Reverend Featherstone," I replied calmly. "Though I suspect that what is out of favor these days is bigotry."

There was a general murmur of disapproval at the table.

"Dad, this is not the occasion," Colin warned. I didn't wonder that he was conflicted with parents such as these.

"No, son, if we allow God's will to be sullied then the world is doomed to damnation. If the good men of the world stand idly by and watch God's commandments trashed then we are no better than they are." For emphasis he actually pointed toward me on 'they.'

If I hadn't already had a mouthful of soup, I would have responded myself but Troy got in before me.

"Everyone is entitled to their own opinion Reverend Featherstone whether it's right or wrong but I fail to see how provoking an argument at a dinner in honor of Marcie's wedding is the appropriate occasion."

Cora Featherstone was indignant. "Provoke?"

"Well, your husband did start it," Troy said quietly.

Featherstone placed his hand on his wife's arm to quiet her. "It was provocation enough that Satan encouraged this sodomite to turn up to sup with us."

Even Marcie joined the fray now. "I'm afraid Satan is not to blame for daddy being here. That was my doing, Reverend Featherstone. I wanted him here for the wedding."

One up for Marcie. Her mother, however, was smirking behind her spoonful of soup.

"Be that as it may. Marcie, an unrepentant sodomite is an affront to God-fearing people the world over."

The stricken look on Colin's face pleaded with me to keep his secret.

"And what if, say for argument's sake, one of your children or grandchildren turned out to be gay?" I asked.

"We have been blessed with but the one child," Featherstone said, his head bowed as if it was with deep regret. "We hope to be blessed with many grandchildren. However, if any of them showed the slightest tendency toward perversion, we would cast them out as God commands."

"Just a minute," Troy interrupted. "Don't you have something to say about this Colin?"

Featherstone answered for him. "Colin does not have his own opinion, Troy, he has only God's opinion."

"Hold your horses here a second," Marcie said.

"Be quiet, Marcie," Melinda snapped.

"I will not be quiet," she said petulantly. I'm sure she would have stamped her foot if she could have.

"See what you've done," Melinda sniped across the table at me.

"Excuse me, Melinda, but none of this is Mr. Flanagan's doing," Troy said. "The Reverend Featherstone is alone responsible for ruining this meal." He pushed his plate aside in disgust.

Featherstone seemed pleased with his handiwork, merely holding his hands in front of him in a prayer position. "I started nothing; I'm merely God's messenger."

"Then He needs to use a different delivery service," Troy said.

All eyes turned to Marcie as she stood, knocking her chair over, drawing herself up to her full height, pointing an accusing finger at Featherstone and his appalled wife. "Don't you dare. Don't you fucking dare think you can interfere in the way Colin and I run our family. It is none of your business how our children turn out. Don't tell me I will disown my own child if he or she turns out to be gay. Okay, I probably won't like it but…" She faltered. In her frustration she punched Colin who sat there like a statue as he watched his whole life crumble around him. "Don't just sit there like a fuckin' rock, Colin. Say something. Grow some balls."

Melinda pulled on Marcie's arm. "Sit down. Stop making a spectacle of yourself."

"Oh, mum, it's not me who's making an idiot of themselves. You only wanted me to invite dad to the wedding so you three could humiliate him. I can see it now. What? You got something planned for the wedding reception? Or the church? You gonna tar and feather him? Run him out of town?" The guilty look on the Featherstone's faces revealed the truth of what she was saying. "You fuckin' hypocrites. You were going to use my wedding to score points. Fuck you, mum. Fuck you, Cora. And a special fuck you, Reverend Featherstone. You're all a pack of cunts."

Even Troy was gobsmacked by the performance although I thought it would probably make him even more in love with her. A few seconds later the hubbub began, everyone talking over the top of everyone else: the Featherstone's demanding an apology, Mel bemoaning the foul language, Troy enthusing about Marcie's stand for independence. Only Colin and I remained mute. I watched him as he struggled with his conscience. He looked to me for help. I winked, and then nodded. I hoped he would make the right decision. He stood slowly while the babble went on around him. Slamming his hand down on the table hard enough to make the plates and cutlery rattle, he shouted, "Be quiet."

Those standing sat immediately, Marcie righting her chair. I noticed Troy had a huge grin on his face. He was enjoying himself immensely. I knew Flax would clap his hands in delight when I told him the story once I got back home. I would have been enjoying the Featherstone's discomfort more had I known what Colin was about to say.

"I've listened to all the bullshit that's been sprouted around the table this evening..."

"Language," Cora whispered.

"Yes, mum, I use those words on occasion, plus a lot of others that would make you fall to your knees in horror." She mumbled a short prayer begging God's forgiveness for his sins. She'd need an industrial-strength prayer for Colin's major transgression.

"But that's not what this is all about." He turned to Marcie and took her hand. "Marcie. I was never more proud of you than I have been tonight. You showed more gumption, more balls if you like, than I have in my entire life. But I hope to remedy that now. Marcie, I can't marry you. I'm not the man for you."

There was a communal gasp as that revelation was the one thing those at the table least expected. Troy surreptitiously moved his chair closer to Marcie.

"There's a man here," Colin continued, "Who loves you infinitely more than I ever could. He will make you the best husband in the world. He's kind, he's loving, and his heart has been yours since we were all children together. Only the ambition of our parents has stopped you from seeing it. Troy, I hope you can convince her that you are so much more worthy of her love than I am." Troy dared to put his arm across the back of Marcie's chair. Colin disentangled Marcie's hand from his own. She tried to take it back but he turned away from her.

"Mum, dad, I was sorry to hear the poison you spruiked tonight, using the Bible as justification for your own hatred and bigotry. I'm ashamed for you, and for you, too, Melinda, for attempting to use our wedding for revenge. But, mum, dad, what I'm about to say will test you in ways you never expected to be tested. It will test whether you love your bigotry more than your son."

I heard a quiet groan from Cora.

"There is someone I love more than my reputation, more than my career, more than my own family if I'm forced to make that choice. That's why I can't marry you, Marcie. We met just over a month ago and over a weekend of the most wonderful passion, passion the like of which I never knew existed before, I fell in love." He paused and I could hear him swallow nervously. "I had no idea at the time my weekend lover was Marcie's father."

All eyes turned in my direction. Cora's groan became a sob of despair.

"Call it luck, call it providence, call it what you will, but when he turned up here today, I knew I couldn't go on with the sham of my marriage. It wasn't fair to Marcie and it wasn't fair to Rich. I tried, Marcie, really I did, but it's not in me to love a woman. Especially not when there's a man like Rich around. Rich? I'm hoping I haven't been presumptuous, but…"

I cut him off by striding around the table to envelop him in my arms and plant the most passionate kiss of my life on his lips.

I heard a 'woo hoo' from Troy while Marcie gasped, "OMG, that is so fuckin' hot." Troy was stopped after another 'woo' and I had to assume Marcie was so turned on she grabbed the nearest hot man for a kiss.

Suddenly I felt strong arms attempt to pull Colin and me apart. It was Featherstone. "Get home, son. Now. We'll pray this evil out of you. Beat it out of you if necessary. We can defeat the devil's handiwork."

"It isn't evil, dad. It's love. Even though it's only in its early stages I hope it will lead to something long lasting and that I might be able to spend the rest of my life with Rich. If he'll have me."

He needed reassurance, so I said, "My home and my heart are yours, Colin."

Featherstone huffed and puffed and in the end said what I expected, "If you leave with this man, Colin, God will turn his back on you. And not just God, so will your mother and I. We will not have perversion in our home."

I wasn't sure that Cora was quite as convinced of that argument as her husband. Given time, I thought she would thaw, especially as Colin was their only child.

"I was hoping you'd understand, dad. I was wrong."

"You are dead to us," Featherstone ranted.

I put a comforting arm around Colin's shoulder. "Troy, Marcie, after such a momentous evening, how about we adjourn to my hotel for a late supper?"

Troy answered first. "We'd love to."

Marcie hit him playfully on the arm. "Don't you go answering for me, Troy Staples. I'm not married to you yet. In fact, I'm not sure I ever will be. You have no prospects, and a girl needs prospects. In fact, I may go and live with daddy and his new lover."

The look of horror on my face must have given me away.

"Just joshing," she laughed. "But you gotta keep these men on their toes."

Colin turned to his father. "I'll pick up a few items on my way past. If you ever change your mind, you can find out where we live through Marcie. I'm sure now she'll be in regular touch with her dad."

Featherstone was adamant. "We won't change our mind."

Colin leaned down to kiss his mother and she wrapped her arms around him so tightly I thought she might crush him. She turned to me when Colin finally extricated himself from her grip and said softly, "Take good care of Colin."

"It won't work out," Featherstone said as a last ditch effort. "You'll be back, begging God's forgiveness. Mark my words."

"Doesn't matter if it doesn't last," Colin replied. "This is what I am. This is what I always will be. This is what God made me."

There was a roar of anger from Featherstone but his wife held him back as we all made a hasty exit.

I couldn't resist one last barb. "Don't think it's been lovely seeing you again, Mel, it hasn't. But, hey, let's do it again in, say, sixty or seventy years."

Outside, Troy and Marcie drove off to the hotel where we were meeting in the bar. They were already arguing like an old married couple.

Colin was understandably quiet as we drove to his parents place in his car. He packed hurriedly, choosing only those items he could fit into two suitcases, leaving behind most of his casual clothes, but taking items of sentimental value. He took one suit for job interviews and a number of college yearbooks. Finally, he took one last look around his old room, extracted a wad of notes from his wallet and stuffed them in a jar above the refrigerator in the kitchen. "Mum's rainy day money," he said. After he turned to drag the cases to the door, I quickly slipped my business card under the cash.

Back at the hotel, Colin excused himself to go to my room. He was hurting but he wanted time alone. I kissed him. "I love you, Colin," I reiterated. "You've made me the happiest man in the world tonight. Never doubt you've made the right decision."

Marcie kissed him on the cheek. "You bastard. Thank God, you didn't leave me at the altar."

Colin went to shake hands with Troy who pulled him in for a bear hug. "Thanks, mate. You got yourself a great man there. Take care of him."

I went up to the room with Colin, tucking him into bed, kissing him sweetly and assuring him I would be back soon. He was already snoring by the time I left. I knew from experience that coming out to your parents is emotionally draining no matter how they take it.

Downstairs, Marcie, Troy and I found a booth and sat in quiet contemplation while the waiter brought our drinks and snacks.

"Why don't you bring your figures and calculations over tomorrow afternoon, Troy, and I'll go over them with you," I suggested. "I might even be able to help you a little financially."

"Wow, would you really do that? That's so cool."

"Not that fatties gym thing again?" Marcie complained.

"I think it's a great idea," I said.

Marcie screwed up her nose, "Really? Eww."

Troy was going to have some task in breaking down her resistance to get her to marry him. It wouldn't happen overnight but if anyone could do it, he could. And from her extraordinary behavior at dinner, I thought there just might be something about Marcie worth Troy's pursuit.

"OMG!" Marcie howled, interrupting my thoughts. "I just thought of something. My ex-groom is about to become my father-in-law."

SUMMER AT RAINBOW COVE

I missed my babe, Tina, from the moment we said our goodbyes at the airport. She and her family were headed to Europe, while I'd drawn the short straw and had a wait of a few hours before I took off for my summer holiday gig as a lifeguard at a luxury island resort off the Sunshine Coast. It was not an amicable goodbye. Tina was being wrenched from my arms by her family – mainly her dad – who thought she was throwing her life away on a no-good bum who had no skills and would never amount to anything. That would be me.

How wrong could the dude be? For starters, I had a world's best in tanning. My bronzed skin was the envy of other dudes in the surfing fraternity. But, I'll let you in on a little secret, it's genetics not some special skill I picked up that enabled me to turn my flesh the color of buttered toast. All I had to do to achieve perfection was to head out to the beach in shorts or Speedos and by the time I came home, bingo, the sun had done all the work. Sweet.

Okay, I guess I didn't have many prospects but, fuck me, I was nineteen years old, what do you want? Still plenty of time to decide on a career, get the training, and settle in for the rest of my life. Nah, not good enough, according to Tina's old man, so he was kidnapping her in order that she couldn't see me during the gap between high school and university. Uni for her, not sure what it would be for me. Maybe an apprenticeship to a motor mechanic. If the world was fair – which it's not – I could have worked all that out while slumming in what's left of the old world with my woman. But, no, Tina's dad wanted to open her eyes to a world without me, whereas she usually only wanted to open her eyes to my dick: a fuckin' work of art. Thick like sausage, long like a snake, and shoots like a repeater.

Six fuckin' months without her hot twat. I'd have blue balls by the time she returned. Well, maybe not. Yeah, I'd promised I'd be a good boy but while the hen's away the cock will... In fact, Tina was adamant that I keep my very generous dimensions in my undies. I worked out later it was probably her that signed me up to a contract for a lifeguard's job at an island resort.

Either her or her old man, or both of them together. I knew she was jealous of my power over other chicks, but a resort? What was she thinking? There'd be beach-to-beach babes just panting for it. I didn't swear fidelity, just that I loved her. There's a world of difference.

The separation wouldn't be as hard on me as I had first imagined. My nights would be full of babes helping me get over my loneliness while, during the day, I'd be perfecting my tan without the help of a spray gun. Chicks would be purring to look on my magnificence every chance they got.

I didn't know what she'd done until I received an email with the electronic ticket attached. I'd been surfing one of my favorite porn sites when it arrived. I thought it might be a message from one of the chicks I was net-flirting with – she'd promised to send me a pussy shot – so I jumped on it when it came through.

"What the fuck?" I mumbled.

It's not easy to read when you got your dick in your hand so I tucked it away, fascinated by this big sparkly CONGRATULATIONS, each letter pulsing in a different color of the rainbow. My first thought was that it was another one of those giveaways from an online casino. You know, 'Here's a free twenty dollars, now start spending until we have your last week's wages, the papers to your car, and a debt that would pay your way to the Bahamas...'

No, the email read: 'Dear Mr. Cody, Congratulations. You're a winner! You have been chosen from the many hundreds of applications we received to become a valued member of the Rainbow Cove staff. For six months, you will live in Paradise courtesy of Rainbow Cove Inc., managers of the country's most prestigious and most sought after playground for those with the taste and desire to mingle with people of a like mind. Your response to our questionnaire, as well as the candid photographs we required, put you in the exclusive one per cent of the population that we are looking for. Your web interview impressed us to the extent we are now activating that clause in your contract that binds you to the resort for six months.

'You'll be sharing one of our exclusive staff cabins on the beach with another of our hand-picked staff. All meals, entertainment and accommodation are yours to enjoy with our compliments. Any alcoholic beverages will be at your own expense which will be deducted each week before your wages are deposited in the bank. We're sure you will enjoy your time with us. Many of our staff choose to stay with Rainbow Cove Resort at the end of their term of employment. We do hope you will consider this as an option when your time comes. Welcome to the Rainbow Cove family.'

I had to read the message three times before it sank in that I had a job for the next six months. A fuckin' half a year. No way. I didn't sign any contract. I don't recall doing an interview. What was this shit? Must be Tina's little joke.

It wasn't. An airline eticket was attached with instructions on where to wait for the bus to take me to the private catamaran once I'd arrived at the airport in the nearest coastal city to the island resort. Also attached was a copy of my contract. Yes, it was my signature. I might have to change it because someone was excellent at forgery. I stopped briefly at the list of my duties. They were easy. I could shit 'em in. I was to be a one of a dozen lifeguards at the resort. What took my breath away was the salary. The money was good. Who am I kidding? The money was fuckin' brilliant. I guess it meant I'd have to put up with a lot of hassles and bullshit from the holidaymakers. They'd have to be wealthy dudes and dudettes because the resort was mega-expensive. Hollywood actor types stayed there. It was more money than I'd earn anywhere apart from performing brain surgery or selling my ass on a street corner. Maybe I could skip the job after three months and head for Europe to catch up with Tina.

The whole idea was beginning to look like a message from the gods. I could do this. Maybe someone was looking out for me, after all. My only concern, and it was minor as far as I was concerned, was that I remembered none of the application process.

Natch, Tina was thrilled that I had a job. She denied knowing anything about it. She didn't seem to be lying. I can usually read Tina like a book. I'm not saying she's shallow just she's about as deep as a Little Golden Book for under-fives.

After the surprisingly tear-free farewell from my beloved and her obnoxious family, who chose to pass through security absolute eons before their plane left, I had enough time to grab a burger and fries. It was odd, while I sat and watched people lugging suitcases to check-in counters, families attempting to keep their kids in check, and tearful lovers wishing each other goodbye, I could have sworn I saw my big brother Rhett heading for the overseas departure gate. Couldn't be. He was spending the summer holidays boning up on his university work. He was gonna be a hotshot lawyer, like Tina's old man. In fact, his academic record was so shit hot, Tina's dad had already offered Rhett an internship if he graduated with the sort of academic record he'd scored thus far. Way to show me up, bro.

I got up out of my seat to call or go after him, but he'd already disappeared through the entry point. Nah, couldn't be. He didn't have enough cash to take himself to a decent restaurant let alone afford to fly overseas.

Unless he got a great deal on one those trips to Bali or New Zealand. I flipped open my mobile and pressed his contact number. It went to voicemail. Not surprising. I guess my imagination was playing tricks on me.

Time went by pretty fast and I was soon boarding my own flight. Nowhere near as exotic as heading to Paris like Tina, but I wasn't complaining; it had cost me zilch. I'd tried Tina on her mobile but she wasn't answering. She told me she'd be buying a new sim card once she hit Paris because the global roaming charges on her Aussie phone would likely bankrupt her dad, especially as we were expecting to spend a lot of time cooing at each other across the thousands of lonely kilometers that separated us. If she was concerned that I'd be sticking my dick in every stray pussy that came my way, I was more concerned that she'd be having such a great time she'd forget about me back at home. I guess that's what her dad was hoping.

I tried Rhett again but he still wasn't answering. That was okay; he needed to get his head around some pretty amazing stuff. I asked him about it once but it made my toes curl with boredom. I didn't understand a word between all the habeas and corpus.

I relaxed into my window seat for the two and a half hour flight. The plane was only half full so I was hoping to get a free seat next to me, not that I could stretch out and sleep or anything, it's just I hate being cramped by those overweight bastards who take up all the elbow room. Looking around, I noticed a lot of good-looking dudes who seemed to be traveling solo. Surfers? Nah, too presentable, not scruffy enough. Surfers usually traveled in packs. And by road.

Slowly the plane filled, although empty seats were dotted around the cabin, the one next to me included. Sweet relief. Then, just as the cabin doors were about to close, this flurry – yeah, flurry is the only word to describe him – panted up the aisle. I could smell the cologne before he even reached my row. He paused, looked at the numbers on his ticket, squashed his carry-on luggage in the overhead locker, and then slumped down next to me before strapping his seat belt around his slim waist.

"I didn't think I was going to make it," he gasped. "Let me catch my breath and I'll introduce myself."

Absolutely no need, I thought.

I prayed he'd read my mind or get the hint from my body language. No such luck. The cabin crew went through the safety ritual as the plane taxied to the runway. I kept my head buried in the flight magazine that was full of adverts for perfumes, electronic goods, and booze. I glanced at my companion who seemed to be gripping the armrest with enough force to turn his knuckles white. He watched the safety demonstration with such terror, I wondered if he may have a heart attack at any moment. I felt sorry for the guy. He was slightly older than me, pretty good looking but with girly features. Body looked solid enough from what I could see from his ill-fitting clothes. I know they tell you to wear loose shirts and trousers on a flight but he'd gone to extremes.

I tried to assure him. "Relax. Take a deep breath. It's the safest way to travel."

"It's not that," he said. "I think I've just made the biggest mistake of my life. If I think about it, I'll tell them to stop the plane and let me off."

I laughed. "You're not old enough to have made the biggest mistake of your life yet, dude."

"Dude? Seriously?" He turned to look at me. "Say, you're cute. Very cute."

I'm pretty sure his eyes were undressing me. I coughed. "I don't even let my girlfriend look at me like that."

"You're straight?"

"You're gay?"

We both laughed.

"I'm not going to have to make an appointment with a dental surgeon to have my teeth removed from the back of my throat?" he asked.

"You must get that a lot if you're so bloody pushy."

"Yeah, right. Like you don't hit on girls all the time."

"Yeah, but that's different."

"Why?"

I didn't even stop to think. "Come on, it's natural."

Before I even realized what I'd said, he'd pressed the button for one of the cabin crew, folded his arms across his chest, and played silent with me. He was worse than Tina.

A few minutes later, one of the male flight crew came along the aisle. "What can I do for you?" he said to my companion although he was appraising me.

What is it with faggots?

"Like what you see?" I sneered.

The guy in the seat next to me said "Is there somewhere I can move. I'm allergic to homophobes."

Again with my mouth. "And I'm allergic to faggots that are so obvious I expect to see wings sprout from their backs. So, fuck you, Tinker Bell."

The male trolley dolly clucked sympathetically. "I see your problem. Come with me, I'll find you somewhere more pleasant to sit." While my ex-seat mate retrieved his bag from the overhead locker, the hissy cabin steward informed me, "No more alcohol for you for the remainder of the flight."

I'd been looking forward to a few free beers. "Hey, I haven't had any yet."

"Well, isn't that a shame? Maybe next time you'll think twice before you run off at the mouth with anti-gay slurs."

I thought I'd try to beat the ban. I signaled to one of the female cabin crew as she passed, giving her my best flirt. "Could I get a beer, please?"

Her mouth curled up like she'd been sucking lemons. "Tea, coffee, water, or soft drinks. What'll it be?"

If she hadn't been such a bitch I might have taken her up to the first-class toilet and given her a taste of my cock. "Nothing for now," I said.

The flight proved to be the longest 150 minutes of my life. They even managed to 'misplace' my lunch. I'd asked about it three times, to be told 'Be patient. It's coming.' Not sure where it was coming from but it still hadn't arrived three months later. Moral: don't piss off the cabin crew on a flight. Even the female flight attendants avoided me. Normally, I left a plane with a fistful of phone numbers. All I got this time was the cold shoulder.

I couldn't get off the flight fast enough when we landed. Waiting at the baggage counter, I noticed all the good-looking guys were chatting amiably in a large group which included Tink, my former seat companion. He was obviously sprouting off because a number of men turned to glare at me, including one enormous muscle dude who would give me serious competition if he was headed to Rainbow Cove. I could breathe easy, that was about as likely as…

My bag swung past on the carousel and I grabbed it, heading over to a guy holding up a cardboard sign with glittery lettering that proclaimed my destination. He asked my name and then marked it off on a sheet attached to a clipboard. "I'm your official greeter, Chris Flanders."

I nodded. "I'm not the only one you're expecting?"

The guy looked me over. "No, there's a few more. The boss likes to get everyone together at the same time." His appraisal complete, he added. "If you don't mind my saying so, you're not the usual look we get at Rainbow Cove."

"I don't mind, but is that a good or a bad thing."

"Neither," he replied. "Just saying."

"What's the usual look?"

He opened his mouth to respond but just then a gaggle of men – the same one that had looked at me as if I was neck deep in doo doo – descended on us, pushing me aside.

"Okay, gents, one at a time. Once you're all marked off, we'll head to the minibus that will take us to the wharf for the boat trip over. I hope you all had a pleasant journey…" He paused for the usual shout of approval but, instead, the entire party turned toward me. "I see," he continued. "When we reach the island, you'll be taken to the meet-and-greet for lunch where Mr. Franklin, the man in charge of your lives for the next six months, will give you the list of regulations. It's pretty basic so no need to panic. Rainbow Cove is all about having fun, relaxing, being yourself among likeminded folk."

I don't know why his speech didn't ring alarm bells; it should have. I put it down to the deep freeze I felt coming from the group. I wondered what the hell Tink had said about me. And why would he be employed at such a ritzy resort, he was a fuckin' screamer. I noticed that a few of the bigger guys with muscles bulging out of their casual shirts sported a rainbow on their biceps. I'm all for ink on the skin, but I thought that was taking brand loyalty a bit too far. That was tongue-up-the boss's-asshole territory.

You ever felt like a pariah? Well, that was me on the bus. No one spoke to me and any time I looked around at the fifteen or so guys in the group, Mr. Muscles put a protective arm around Tink. They didn't bother introducing themselves to me although I noticed everyone else seemed to be on first-name terms.

Chris Flanders kept up a running commentary as we headed from the airport toward the coastal city where, he said, "You'll get a week off every eight weeks and the boat will take you from the island to the mainland and pick you up at the end of your stay. We find most of our staff prefer to remain on the island because of the quality of the food, the fact we have the latest movies and TV series on demand, plus staff have their own private beach area, and, of course, there's the company of fellow staff members. Although we don't encourage fraternization between staff members and especially between staff and guests, we know it can be a lonely and frustrating time for many of you and the inevitable will happen."

That was the best news I'd heard all day. Not only could I fuck the female staff with impunity, but also the guests. My dick was gonna be working overtime. I guess my grin said it all because Flanders turned on me. "That does not, however, Mr. Cody, mean that you're free to treat your fellow staff members or the guests as your own personal smorgasbord."

The men on the bus laughed at my discomfort.

The town we passed through on the way to the wharf looked respectable enough although it had delusions of grandeur if it considered itself a city. It was no bigger than some of the smaller suburbs where I came from. The streets were busy enough, though hardly congested, and there seemed to be a plentiful array of good shops and eateries, plus the ubiquitous shopping mall which would almost certainly have a food court that served 'Foods of the World' that would consist mainly of sushi, Thai, Chinese, Lebanese, American, and Italian cuisine. There was a cinema megaplex with five theatres, plenty of pubs, and even a casino.

"If you want to lose your hard-earned wages, that's the place to go," Flanders said, pointing to the casino. "The odds are stacked against you so, please, try not to be foolish. There is no casino at the resort." A number of men groaned. "Gentlemen, I know a lot of you are here to stash as much money aside for your university fees or pay off some debt. I wouldn't be surprised if one or two of you were on the lam from drug runners or the cops…" He waited for the laugh before continuing. "But I do have to warn you at this juncture, although management tolerates recreational substances among the guests, it is frowned upon amongst the staff. What is totally prohibited is an array of hard drugs for everyone at Rainbow Resort. Mr. Franklin will elaborate at your luncheon. We're not wowsers, but we do insist on a certain standard from our employees."

Not a problem for me, for apart from beer and the occasional toke, my body is a temple. It looked as if the guys on the bus were reading from the same page.

It was a warm day and the slow journey, together with Flanders' voice, lulled me to sleep. Before I nodded off, I noticed a few of the others were getting a kip, so I didn't feel guilty. The whoosh of the bus's mechanical door opening woke me. There was an air of excitement now as we were next to the marina where multi-million dollar yachts were moored, tantalizing our luxury taste buds. I picked out at least three of the vessels that would suit my personality. I'd make it a task to see if any of those fine yachts was owned by a woman. There must be one or two. I could play toy boy for a week to get my hands on a sleek runabout.

Feel guilty? Why? Tina was off on the journey of a lifetime, so why not enjoy myself in her absence. I just wished her old man owned one of these boats because I'd make it my duty to punch a hole below the waterline so it sank into the mud. Not that I was bitter.

"This way, gentlemen," Flanders called, bursting our maritime dreams.

As we made our way along the waterfront toward the modern wood and glass structure that served as the ferry terminal for the vessels to the small hamlets dotted among the islands off the coast, Tink was directly ahead. I knew what I had to do to. I caught up to him and Mr. Muscles who seemed to have adopted him.

"Look," I said quietly so as not to attract other people's attention. "I owe you an apology. I'm sorry. What I said was insensitive."

Tink agreed. "You think?"

Muscles was watching with interest as we kept walking toward the catamaran waiting at the wharf. "Let me make it up to you somehow."

"How?" Tink asked.

"I don't know—"

"You could suck his dick," Muscles interrupted.

I almost lost it. "What the fuck? Are you his pimp or something?"

Tink looked at me as if he suddenly realized something. "You really are straight?"

What parallel universe were these people from? "Do I look the slightest bit gay to you?"

Tink shrugged. "I thought you were just one of those self-hating queers who don't like anyone who's obvious."

"Totally S.T.R.A.I.G.H.T."

Muscles smirked. "Give the man a lollipop, he can spell."

"Nah, I bet he doesn't suck lollipops," Tink said. "It would be too emasculating for him to put something the shape of a cock in his mouth."

"Okay. Look, I said I was sorry. I don't know what else I can say or do, but obviously an apology is not enough. I tried."

Muscles looked at me as if I'd suddenly grown an extra head. "How did you get this job? Their application process is stringent."

"I don't even remember applying. I have a sneaking suspicion my girlfriend's dad sent the application. Forged my signature."

"That doesn't explain how you got past the one-on-one interview," Tink added.

"I never did one."

"Strange," Muscles said. "Do you have a twin?"

"Nah. Just an older brother." The penny dropped. "Shit! I've been set up."

Tink looked as if he felt sorry for me. "They really must hate you." I guess I was puzzled and it showed. "You have no idea what Rainbow Cove Resort is all about, do you?"

"Not a clue," I admitted.

Muscles hooted with laughter. "Hoo, boy. I want to be there when you find out."

What the hell was going on? Had I fallen asleep and woken up in some bizarre reality television program? I looked about for cameras, anything to give me an inkling of my predicament.

I let Tink and Muscles get ahead again before following on. Fuck Tink for not accepting my apology. No, he'd probably enjoy that. Without even instructing my eyes what to do, I glanced at his ass. Men's asses are shaped differently to women's. No, I'm not a moron, I knew that fact, but I'd never really thought about it. Now that I looked, really looked, at another dude's butt, I noticed it had a beauty all its own. Tink's was curvy; at least what I could see of it outlined in his baggy trousers. Now, Muscles', that was an ass. He must work out because his tight jeans showed off that bubble butt to perfection. I bet he had chicks drooling over it. It was some booty. I guess if I was a gay guy, I'd want to sink my hot, hard cock between those ass cheeks until I dumped a load way up inside him.

WTF! What was I thinking? I shook my head to dislodge these unwanted thoughts. When did I start appraising a man's ass as somewhere to sink my dick? Especially Muscles' ass. If he could read my mind he'd probably rip my head off with those powerful arms of his.

Tina, come back.

The trip over on the catamaran should have been uneventful. I was being shunned still, so I was staring off at the city as it grew smaller the farther we traveled. I wondered if I would have been better served remaining there and allowing the others to depart without me. My head was a mass of contradictions, forcing me to suppress things I really didn't want to think about just then. Things such as Tina, my brother Rhett at the airport because I was now convinced it was him I spotted, and what the hell was going on at Rainbow Cove that Muscles seemed to think was so funny?

I heard the excitement as the island hove into view. Rainbow Cove Resort was but a small part of the island although it was the only inhabited section; the remainder was bush and sand kept as wild as possible for the small amount of native wildlife, meaning there were a few no-go areas, the remainder fenced off for bush walks. I turned to look at what would be my home for the next six months. I whistled in appreciation. The brochures and photos on the web just didn't do it justice. It did, indeed, look like fuckin' paradise.

All my doubts and fears disappeared. I was eager to get on with it, although I had no idea as yet what 'it' involved apart from my job description as 'lifeguard.' In Australia the difference between lifesaver and lifeguard was the difference between voluntary work and paid employment. I was definitely in the paid category.

The hotel rose majestically in a flat area set back from the yellow sands of the beach, protected from the wilder elements by the cove. Hills rose to the back of the complex, and about a mile to the left of the main building was a waterfall, obviously man-made because as far as my reading revealed, there were no rivers on the island. It cascaded in a spectacular fall that would kill anyone who attempted to ride down it. There was also an enormous swimming pool on the right side of the complex, obviously for those who didn't wish to brave the surf.

The hotel itself blended seamlessly with its surroundings, almost hidden in parts by the luxuriously appointed trees that dotted the verdant lawns. I wondered if they were artificial. Although the building was designed to ape the countenance of Europe's grand hotels, it still had modern touches such as the glass elevators that rose up the sides of the vast twelve-story structure. There was also a glass enclosed atrium dead center at the hotel entrance. As we got closer to the island we could see internal lifts carrying passengers from floor to floor like busy worker bees, men in livery delivering drinks to people lounging in groups, while a pianist played on the ground floor. I felt totally out of place.

The arm placed around my shoulder shook me from my day dreams. It was Muscles. My immediate response was not to shake his arm off but to appreciate his strength. This was a guy you'd want as a buddy. A guy I definitely wanted to know better.

"Listen, mate," he said, "Much as the two of us think you're a prize asshole, we couldn't let you get off the boat clueless."

"I guess I was a bit hard on you," Tink said, then giggled at his double entendre.

I was cautious. "Okay."

"You sticking to your story you have no idea what Rainbow Cove is all about?" Muscles asked. I nodded. "You don't know what the symbolism of the rainbow some guys have inked on their arms?"

"I thought they were sucking up to management."

"Oh, dude. You are so naïve."

"Much as I'd love to see you fall on that delectable ass of yours…" Tink waited for my reaction to his comment about my ass. I wasn't biting. "Hm, no reaction. I guess that's a slight improvement, although I was hoping you'd say 'Kiss my ass' and I would have been down on my knees so fast you wouldn't have seen me until you felt my tongue in your crack."

"Stop it," Muscles said. "Don't confuse the man."

"Go on then, tell him. It'll sound better coming from you than me."

Muscles squeezed my shoulder as if he were a great mate of long standing. I don't know why, but I liked the feel of the guy. He gripped my shoulder in a mock comradely fashion, took a deep breath, and asked, "Are you ready for this dick-for-brains? Rainbow Cove is a gay resort. There the secret's out."

The look of amazement on my face must have said it all. "Gay?"

Tink helped me out. "That's where one male inserts Tab A into another male's Slot B."

I shrugged Muscle's arm off. "I know what gay means. It means I'm well and truly fucked."

"Not yet, but give it time," Muscle's smirked.

"Not gonna happen. Ever," I spat, still attempting to get my head around the revelation. "You mean all those guys on the plane—"

"G.A.Y." Tink interrupted.

I turned to Muscle's. "You're...?"

"Come on, dude, and try real hard to comprehend the enormity of your predicament. All the guests and staff at Rainbow Cove are either gay as glitter or at least the gay side of bi. It's a smorgasbord of man-on-man lovin'. You'll be the only straight dude on the island. That means your popularity will sky rocket."

I screamed, "What have they done to me?" Yeah, you read that right. Mr. Straight-and- Definitely-Not-Bi-Curious working amongst faggots.

That's why Tina signed me up. She realized I'd have no one to siphon my ball juice cause there was no way a dude was gonna be munching on my knob, and someone would get seriously injured if they tried anything on my ass. Tina once tried putting her finger up my date; she had a black eye for a month. Nah, I didn't hit her but my reaction was so severe I brought my knee up and caught her in the face. Something else that didn't endear me to her family. Not that they knew she was giving me a blow job when she got it, although I think her dad suspected.

Tink was more sympathetic. "You really didn't know? This is not some ruse to get more ass than the rest of us?"

"Do I look as if I shag men's shitholes?"

"Oooh, get Mr. Sensitive," Tink minced.

"You might want to turn down the homophobic outbursts a notch or two," Muscles suggested. "Especially if you want to keep the job."

I was exasperated so my voice was getting louder and more hysterical. "Why would I want to keep a job amongst a load of faggots?"

Tink just looked daggers at me before storming off. "You're beyond help."

"Look, mate," Muscles said. "You may be as straight as you pretend but there's no need to be an asshole about it. It's time for you to clench those cute butt cheeks of yours, man up, and tell the boss of Rainbow Cove there's been some mistake and get the fuck off the island if gay men are that repulsive to you. Otherwise, learn to relax, enjoy the resort, no one is forcing you to suck dick, or take a juicy hard cock up your virgin ass. Hell, you may even learn that gay guys are not much different to you."

I snorted. "Except for the holes you use."

"I don't even begin to understand why that matters to you."

The catamaran had moored at the Rainbow Cove dock and Tink called impatiently, "Come on, we're here. Leave him. Let him wallow in his hetero self-righteousness."

Muscles patted my ass and I'd balled my hand into a fist ready to strike. He laughed at my reaction. "A straight guy who was confident in his masculinity would never react like that, mate. Think about it." He hurried off to join Tink and the other staff while I loitered, contemplating my choices. Eventually one of the crew called, "Hey, mate. The others have all left. Time to get your ass into gear."

"I've changed my mind," I replied. "I'll just stay on board and head back to the mainland with you."

"You'll have quite a wait. There are no more scheduled trips today. Besides, your bag's already been unloaded."

"Shit!"

Mine was the lone suitcase on the dock by the time I disembarked. Some resort, I thought. They don't even send anyone to collect your bags. I picked it up and raced after the rest of the staff who were making their way toward the impressive entrance and the buff, middle-aged gentleman who was greeting them. I was puffing by the time I reached him. Without giving him an opportunity to say a thing, I blurted out, "There's been a terrible mistake."

His look silenced me. "Yes, I can see that," he said quietly. "Those flip flops are a definite faux pas. You must be the much discussed Mr. Cody. Welcome. Though I'm guessing you feel anything but welcome. I'm Trent Franklin, the owner of Rainbow Cove. What's say you and I head along to my office and discuss your future with the resort?"

The only thing I wished to discuss was how to get off the island.

"Leave your bag there, Mr. Cody. No one will steal anything. All my staff are hand-picked and carefully vetted."

I couldn't resist a snort of derision.

He didn't take it personally. "Things can go wrong even in the best of places."

His office was on the ground floor at the back of the hotel, large glass double-doors opening out onto a private courtyard that screamed luxury. Instead of sitting behind his desk, he led me out onto the terrace with views of the rainforest that encroached as if ready to pounce on the small oasis of order carved out by the hotel and resort facilities if anyone so much as turned their back. Franklin pointed to a seat and told me to sit. The scent of forest wildflowers and the sounds of strange birds wafted on the breeze, lulling me into a sort of calm. Franklin noticed. "It has that effect on everyone. That's why Rainbow Cove is so popular."

He handed me a foreign beer which I popped and drank from the can, wiping my mouth on the back of my hand. Franklin contented himself with an Italian sparkling water. "So, let's get down to business, Mr. Cody. We seem to have a dilemma."

I noticed the dilemma was not all mine. Trent Franklin quite liked me. It showed in his expensive tailor-made casual trousers that hugged his body like a jealous lover. I sat on the edge of my seat just in case he tried anything with that blunt instrument wedged in his pants.

Maybe it was a mistake to dress down like I did. You know, baggies and flip flops but I'm a casual sorta guy and it was no use pretending otherwise.

"Quite frankly, Mr. Cody, you're not the usual type of person we have applying for this job." I'd heard that song before. It was getting stale.

I was offhand in my reply because I was offended by his inference that I didn't quite make the grade. I wasn't up to his standards. "Who gives a shit whether the guy dragging you out of the water when you're drowning belongs to right clubs or reads the right newspapers?"

"Do you actually read newspapers, Mr. Cody?" he smirked.

"Look, enough with the Mr. Cody shit. My name's Ty, okay? And if you weren't such a smug, patronizing twat I'd agree with just about everything you're thinking."

He ignored my outburst. "Tell me, why did you apply for this position?"

I told him up front and honest about Tina and her dad, and my suspicions they had applied on my behalf. And that my brother may have been the person he interviewed. "Now that you mention it, and I've had an opportunity to watch you up close, there is a difference. I hope you don't mind my saying so, but you are far less polished than your brother. In your defense, you carry off that rough trade look quite successfully."

"It's not a look, it's me."

He folded his hands, crossed his legs and stared at me for a moment. "Are you telling me you're straight?"

"Damn right, I am."

"Bi curious?"

"Not even remotely inquisitive."

He laughed at that. "Occasionally, we get men apply who are looking for an excuse to 'test the waters' shall we say?"

I was adamant. "That's not me." I was shaking my head so violently it was threatening to fall off.

Franklin looked smug. "Of course, they all say that."

That was it. I was pissed off. No use continuing this conversation. "Sorry to waste your time, but I don't think this is going to work out." A small part of me regretted the loss of the cash and the benefits while a much larger part was glad to be out of this perverts paradise. No point being rude, so I shook the dude's hand before I made my way to the door. He had a puzzled look on his face. "I think there's been some misunderstanding. Please. Come back and sit down."

Shit! The part of me that was doing a Snoopy happy dance was suddenly stifled. I sat down again.

"You're quite a character, Mr. Cody. Rough, rude, unformed. You'll be very popular."

"Huh?"

"We are short one lifeguard already. Chicken pox, I believe. He won't be joining us until much later. Meanwhile, I can't afford to be two lifeguards down. You will remain at the resort until we can find a replacement for you."

"What part of 'I don't want to bloody be here,' don't you understand?"

His voice became like steel. "I understand all of it perfectly well, Mr. Cody. What I don't understand is what part of "You signed a contract and I have you by the balls,' you don't understand." Then he smiled. "Grit your teeth and bear it, Mr. Cody. Think of the money. Think of the trinkets you can buy your girlfriend. If there is one."

He had a point. The money was enough to get me to Europe with a pretty classy engagement ring. That should win over Tina and her dad. Mind, you, I'd have a few things to say about signing me up to this joint. I guess I could forgive her, she was jealous I'd be giving away my gonad juice too freely while she was away and this was her one way of preventing that. Smart girl. Goodbye freedom, hello bulging bank account. I easily fit the bill for what they were seeking in a lifeguard although Franklin warned me I would have to put up with gay flirting. I shrugged. "Not like it will be the first time. As long as the guys keep their hands to themselves, there'll be no problems."

He stood to signify the interview was over. "I'll see you at the little welcoming party shortly. Meanwhile, I suggest you get yourself settled in. You'll find a tag on your suitcase with your cabin number and a map of the resort. I suggest you commit it to memory at your earliest convenience. Welcome to Rainbow Resort."

The hotel was eerily quiet as I padded back along the corridor to my bag. A large cardboard tag declared I was in Cabin 18. Also attached was a full-color laminated lay-out of the island, with a reverse that had the paths and trails of the actual resort mapped out in large print. It was easy to follow, the staff bungalows separated from the main hotel by means of a thicket of rainforest, allowing for privacy. There was an air of excitement as I passed the accommodation, most of the cabins had their doors wide open with men chatting amiably on doorsteps or on the paths. I was given a wide berth as I searched for number 18, wondering who my housemate would be.

My heart sank when I found what was to be my home for the next few weeks, if not months. Tink was standing in the doorway. He looked about as thrilled as I did. "Number 18?" he asked. I nodded. He called into the bungalow. "Hey, guess who you're gonna be sharing with?" Muscles stuck his head around the door. "Maybe you can ask for a swap," Tink suggested.

"Maybe you should mind your own business," I suggested.

"So, you're staying?" Muscles asked.

"I was given no choice. Seems they're already down a lifeguard. They couldn't afford to lose another one."

"Well, I for one am going to lock my door at night. I don't want to be murdered in my bed by the marauding homophobe."

Muscles swatted Tink on the butt. "Behave yourself."

"Get a room, you two," I said.

"Listen to her," Tink sneered. "You're not going to last long if a little banter upsets you. There'll be full on fucking and sucking going on around the pool and on the beach, so you'd better get used to it."

I could see my eyes and my brain would need a good scrub with carbolic every night.

"Which is my room?" I asked.

Muscles pointed. I had to hand it to Franklin, the cabins were well appointed. The bedroom wasn't spacious but was large enough to move about in, had copious amounts of closet space, its own en suite bathroom and toilet, while the cabin itself had a communal living room with flat-screen TV and a Blu-ray player, plus a small kitchenette with full-size refrigerator, a hotplate and a microwave. I could get used to this life, if I wasn't so mad keen on getting away from the you know who's.

There was no time to unpack because we were all summoned to the hotel ballroom for the meet-and-greet session. Muscles pulled me into an arm lock, dragging me along with him and Tink. "Come on, mate. We gotta share a home so we might as well make the most of it." He thrust out his hand and introduced himself, then introduced Tink. I never thought of them by their real names and within two or three weeks, I'd totally forgotten what they were anyway. It wasn't until sometime later when I was called upon to introduce them to another staff member that I blurted out their names as Muscles and Tink to the general amazement of everyone in listening distance. I had a lot of explaining to do.

But that was weeks away. Right then I was more interested in what Trent Franklin had to say. He'd completed his spiel about the brotherhood of Rainbow Cove, the sanctity of privacy for the famous and infamous, and how it was our job to ensure everything ran smoothly. Touching on sexual activity among the staff and patrons, he said he was fairly laid back about it although the company policy did not encourage it because of the fall-out from bad break-ups and jealousy.

Then he added, much to my consternation, "Before I let you all loose on the buffet, I'd like to bring to your attention that one of our lifeguards, Mr. Ty Cody, is straight." He gestured in my direction and all eyes turned to me, a few men hissing their displeasure. "Now, gentlemen, that's a little unfair. Mr. Cody was the victim of a very poor joke by his girlfriend who wanted to ensure his fidelity while she's on an overseas jaunt with her dad. He had no idea that he'd been signed up for a six-month stint in a gay resort. Mr. Cody is one hundred per cent straight, so please make him feel at home for the duration of his stay with us. Under normal circumstances we would have been agreeable to tearing up his contract and returning him to the mainland but we're short of lifeguards and, until we can recruit another one or two, he has agreed to stay to help out."

Agreed? I was threatened.

The buffet went off without a hitch and some of the men who'd treated me as if I had some sort of communicable disease earlier now made an effort to befriend me. I knew part of it was their disbelief that I was straight or else they thought they had enough charm to seduce me to the 'other side,' but a few of them seemed genuinely amused by my predicament. Muscles shadowed me at a distance to ensure there was no trouble while Tink got very chatty and friendly with a remarkably handsome middle-aged man who seemed to be the head waiter.

I called Muscles over. "Hey, dude, thanks for looking out for me but I think you should look after your own. Your boyfriend is getting very pally with that old dude."

He seemed puzzled. "What boyfriend?"

I nodded at Tink who was blinking puppy dog eyes at the older man.

"He's not my boyfriend," Muscles laughed. "We get on great together but he's not my type at all. And I'm not his."

I wanted to ask what his type was but it seemed much too familiar for the short time we'd known each other. I wondered why I cared.

We had a few days to familiarize ourselves with the resort, orientation would begin the next day, but I was keen to get back to Bungalow 18 to unpack, and just relax, maybe sink a few brews, and try to get my head around why Tina or her dad had set me up. I felt odd reporting to Muscles what I was doing but as he'd been in deep conversation with another muscle dude for the good part of half an hour, I didn't want him crashing our communal cabin with his dick hanging out or his mate hard as a rock. That was the excuse I gave myself anyway.

I'd unpacked, stored everything away, explored the kitchen to discover it had been stocked with healthy food items, and that we had a tab at the resort's mini-mart even though there was a staff cafeteria for our meals open 24/7. I was propped up on the comfy lounge chugging a brew when Muscles returned. Alone.

"Hey, dude," I greeted him.

"Hey, yourself."

"What happened to that big bastard you were so up close and friendly with when I left? I thought for sure you were on a winner."

"I have plenty of time to follow up."

I grunted my disapproval. "An opportunity postponed is an opportunity wasted."

"Listen, dickwad, not every gay guy jumps into bed at the first opportunity. Some of us are after a relationship rather than a string of one-night stands." He grabbed himself a beer and joined me on the lounge.

"Shit, you're unnatural, dude. If I was gay and had so many hot available guys within reach I'd be fucking myself stupid."

He smirked. "Would you now?"

"You know what I mean. I was just saying because if all those hot dudes were hot chicks, my cock would get no rest."

Muscles looked at the ceiling as if pleading for help. "How did I manage to be put with such a total charmer?"

We argued over which movie to watch on the cable channel: he wanted a gay rom-com and I wanted an action movie. We compromised. Any time we were home together and wanted to watch TV it would be choice about. I won the toss that time and we settled in for the first of a new supernatural action series titled *Transference*. At the end, Muscles admitted he'd enjoyed the full-on violence and deafening explosions. He spoiled it all by adding, "And that leading man, Jason Gianfranco, is so hot I'd have his babies."

"Gross," I squirmed.

"So it was okay for you to slobber every time the female star came on screen but not okay for me and Jason."

He was right; I just wasn't used to gay guys. "Cut me some slack, dude. This is all new to me."

"You don't have any gay friends, do you?"

"Fuck, no," I answered too quickly without thinking.

He laughed. "The few weeks that you're at Rainbow Cove should be a real eye opener for you then."

It was. My orientation was comparatively easy. I met the other guys hired as lifeguards and they seemed a pretty good bunch. A roster was drawn up. Four of us were on duty at any time, in radio contact with each other and with the resort control center. One duo patrolled the pool area while the other looked after the ocean beach. Easy, especially as I'd been a volunteer lifesaver with one of the top surf clubs back home.

The resort had a state-of-the-art small hospital although for serious injury there was a helicopter on stand-by to transport the patient to the major hospital on the mainland. There was everything that would ever be needed on hand. The job seemed a breeze and I regretted I couldn't stay for the entire six months, particularly as the money would come in handy when I pursued Tina.

I'd connected with her once she'd landed in Paris although she kept fobbing me off when I asked for her new cell phone number saying she hadn't got around to buying the local sim card as yet. Our communication was mainly via Facebook entries which meant hers were very general and aimed at the friends she'd left behind. There was nothing personal for me. The time zone seemed to preclude Skype although I began to get the impression she was avoiding me. I also checked my big bro's Facebook page but it was strangely silent. I didn't bother with too many personal social media updates myself because I didn't want to cop shit from all my mates if they found out where I was working. I uploaded a few generic shots of the resort I'd taken on my mobile; just enough to make people jealous, always careful to avoid getting a rainbow flag in the pic or any of the gay guys who paraded around in sweet fuck all, advertising what they had between their legs or displaying their ass like it was prime pussy.

Yeah, I know if it was chicks doing the same thing I'd be lavish in my praise. Fuck, did I just use the word 'lavish'? See, these gays are getting to me. Muscles explained that you can't catch it, not like herpes or genital warts, but I could pick up a few gay habits that might make me a more sensitive person. Sarcastic bastard. It could only help in the performance of my duties. Of course, it was an open secret that I was the token straight man at the gay resort.

Did I say earlier the job was a breeze? Yeah, well not once it became known that I was unavailable. That was like a red rag to a bull and it got so I was being propositioned at every turn, some guys desperate enough to pretend they were drowning so that I'd jump in and save them or give them mouth-to-mouth. For a fleeting second, as I was working on one really hot guy whose cock strained in his Speedos, I thought the job would be so much easier if I was gay. I was even more popular among these guys than I ever was with chicks, although I guessed that had more to do with my unattainable status.

That's how the first month passed. Me doing my job, sharing the evenings with Muscles who liked nothing better than to wind down at home after a hard day as a fitness instructor. He came back to the bungalow exhausted, complaining about guys hitting on him. "They just won't take 'no' for an answer. I can't begin to imagine what it must be like for you."

I felt particularly edgy at the end of that first month. I'd got used to the propositions, the knowing smirks from the guests as I passed, feeling my Speedo-clad butt, cock, and balls ogled until I thought they'd be singed off with the heat of the stares. I was itchy for some action. I hadn't accumulated enough leave yet to get over to the mainland, I was sick of handling myself in the shower, and Tina's updates had all but abated. I had managed to contact her on Skype once but she looked less than thrilled that I'd managed to get through, cutting the conversation short when her dad called that they were ready to head to the Louvre or some other tourist spot.

When Muscles suggested we let off some steam at the staff disco I rejected the idea at first. "I'm not dancing with some strange dude who'll try to shove his tongue down my throat or grab my balls."

"Then you can dance with me. I promise I won't do any of those naughty things you mentioned."

I considered the offer. What the hell? Dancing with a dude. Me?

Muscles had been a good mate, so I faked it. "Hey, man, I don't want to cramp your style. You've been babysitting me for the best part of a month. You get out there and enjoy yourself. Get yourself laid. You've been acting kind of crabby lately."

Normally, I wouldn't notice if one of my buddies was pissed off or sulking but it was different with Muscles; we shared a home. We were in each other's pockets. We were almost like a husband and…husband. We moaned to each other at the end of the working day. I'd even let Muscles give me one of his massages to ease the tension after a particularly aggressive American tourist would not believe I was straight. "There's no such thing as a totally straight man," he declared as his hand went for my family jewels. I suppose I over-reacted so he reported my behavior to resort management and I'd been hauled over the coals, although it was a mild reprimand because that particular guest had a track record of such behavior.

Muscles was a bona fide masseur and his fingers sure did the trick on my back and shoulders, kneading the stress right out of my body. I could get used to it. I was hopelessly embarrassed though when I turned over because I was sporting an erection. "Don't be shy,"

Muscles laughed, "It doesn't mean you're gay. It happens to everyone. Just relax."

We got along real well most of the time. He pulled me up when he thought my attitudes were Stone Age or when I inadvertently said something that could be construed as hurtful. Through him, I learned to watch my language. I also learned not to take flirtatious behavior so badly and, in fact, I got very good at rebuffing advances so that no one went off with their knickers in a twist. It wasn't difficult to say something along the lines of, "If I ever turn gay, you'll be the first person I get in touch with" although I couldn't say it to everyone. I had a book full of variations on the same theme.

I learned, too, how to pay compliments. It's easy when you get off on the way hot chicks look, although it took more practice finding things to say about gay dudes. Mentioning the curvature of their ass, the package in their budgie smugglers, or how ripped their body looked, or just merely noticing they'd had a haircut or were sporting stubble, seemed to do the trick. I was getting there. Muscles had been a great help all along the way, so when he sighed at my rejection we go to the disco, I knew it was time to pay the debt.

"Okay, but I'm not holding hands with you," I smiled.

We showered, dressed in our hottest clubbing gear although Muscles sent me back to change twice, finally coming in to my bedroom to scrounge through my wardrobe giving up in despair at my lack of good social wear. My idea of smart casual was a new pair of flop flops, a pair of shorts, and a T-shirt.

"Let's see if any of my stuff fits you," he groaned in frustration.

I couldn't believe his closet was packed with clothes for all different occasions. "When's your first break on the mainland?" he asked. When I told him, he looked serious. "Overlaps the last two days of mine. I'll come over on the cat with you and we'll spend a day shopping."

"I don't do shopping," I said.

He raised an eyebrow. "You think I can't tell?" Muscles could be so gay sometimes. "Here, these are a size too small so they might fit you." He handed me a shirt that I normally wouldn't be caught dead in, and a pair of men's casual trousers, but he had no footwear that would fit. "Damn, I guess those loafers of yours that are almost worn through will have to do. With luck, no one will look at your feet. Now get changed. I don't want to be seen at the club with a scruff."

I went back to the bedroom to change. Sure, the clothes were still slightly too large but not so you'd notice. When I was ready I glanced at myself in the mirror just to check my zip was done up – you know, man stuff. Wow, I looked hot. Before I could stop my brain, it said, 'I'd do me.' That meant I'd be receiving a lot of unwanted attention later. Still, it was too late to pull out now, plus I hoped that Muscles being with me would be protection enough.

Muscles and I had spent most of our spare time together, oblivious to all the other social interaction going on around us, except for the occasional visit from Tink who kept us amused with anecdotes about his sex life. He was playing the field but we could both tell he'd set his sights on Sydney, the head waiter, who was pursuing him with a single-mindedness that spoke of infatuation or, just maybe, true love.

We'd even taken to eating in the cabin rather than the cafeteria which had a predominance of food kept lukewarm in bains Marie, heavy in fat and carbohydrates. Muscles was an excellent cook although his preference for healthy foods sometimes left me craving crisps or pizza. When I complained once too often, he made a healthy pizza that made my usual mass produced takeaways taste like cardboard. I couldn't help asking, "Why has some gay dude not snapped you up?"

He shrugged. "I guess I just haven't met the right guy."

"God, this is so good. If I wasn't such a straight bastard, I'd get down on one knee and ask you to marry me. Look at you. Hot body, good looking, you're interested in things, you stay positive, I bet you're good in bed. Wow, I wish there was a pill I could take that would turn me gay just so I could propose to you." I was shocked by what I just said. Another case of my mouth running off with my brain. Muscles looked just as shocked as I was. He mumbled something about needing to do something at the gym and rushed out. It was only then I realized I was hard. WTF?

The staff Rainbow Club – there was a larger, more luxurious version for the guests – was crowded but Muscles must have told Tink we were coming and he'd managed to secure a booth far enough away from the dance floor that we didn't have to shout to be heard. He was holding very tightly to Sydney who looked especially dashing in his casual gear. Tink's possessiveness obviously pleased Sydney who was smirking triumphantly. There was a bottle of champagne in an ice bucket as well as four glasses awaiting our arrival.

"What's the occasion?" Muscles asked.

"Go on, you tell them," Sydney suggested.

For the first time ever, Tink appeared shy. "Sydney and I are gonna give it a go."

"Congratulations," Muscles enthused, reaching across the table to squeeze Tink and Sydney on the arm.

"About time," I grumbled as Sydney poured us each a glass of bubbly. Not my favorite drink but I could put up with it for the occasion. Despite my miserly acknowledgment of their commitment, I was happy for the two of them.

I nudged Muscles. "Your turn next."

"No-one available who's my type." He blushed as he said it.

I was still curious to find out what his type was, so when he got up to head to the men's room to point Percy at the porcelain and grab two beers on his way back, I took the opportunity to quiz Tink. "So what is his type?"

Tink looked amazed. "You don't know?"

"Would I be asking if I did?"

"You, you idiot. You're his type."

I was gob smacked. "Me? But I'm straight."

Tink must have realized he'd said too much because he began to backtrack. "Not you specifically. I mean he likes gay guys who have your look and your sort of body."

"Oh," I said as if I understood. But I didn't. There were lots of guys at the resort who were better looking than me and had better bodies. In fact, working in a gay resort was giving me a bit of a complex.

Fortunately, Sydney changed the subject so by the time Muscles returned our conversation was in neutral territory, although I was still puzzled by Muscles' lack of a boyfriend. Most of the staff had settled into short-term fuck buddy relationships or else something stronger and more long-term. Muscles wasn't even fucking around. Or if he was, he definitely wasn't bringing them home.

We'd developed an easy camaraderie, to the extent that I would sometimes fall asleep on his shoulder or he'd put his head on my thigh while we watching TV. I'd do that with my straight mates sometimes so it seemed only natural when Muscles and me began the same ritual. It also seemed natural when he put his arm up on the top of the vinyl seating behind me and pulled me in for a cuddle.

Tink stared but kept mum about it, although I noticed a buzz went around the club and people began staring. My thoughts about whether we should be so gay intimate under the circumstances were cut short when Muscles stood up and held out his hand. "Come on, let's dance. Let's get some of those knots out of our muscles."

I'm not the world's greatest dancer but it was Muscles asking and I could scarcely refuse, however I wasn't about to let him lead me onto the dance floor. I swatted his hand away. "No touching," I said primly. He laughed, taking no offence at all.

Among the crush of people throwing their bodies about, few people took any notice of us. Even my awkward movements which seemed to tickle Muscles' funny bone went unnoticed by the majority. "Is that how straights dance?" he chuckled.

I pouted. "What's wrong with the way I dance?"

I knew what his answer was going to be before he even said it. "Everything."

He gave me a few basic instructions on ways to move my body, adjusting my actions to iron out bad habits. I liked it when he touched me, eventually relaxing as I got the hang of it.

"That's better," he smiled. I beamed under his compliment.

My mouth had other ideas. "You trying to turn me gay?"

He looked as if I'd slapped him. He left the dance floor without warning. Moody bastard. I'd noticed his rapid change of personality in the past few weeks, wondering if there was a situation he wasn't talking about. He was very private even when we were alone, whereas I'd spilled my guts about Tina at every opportunity.

I followed him back to the booth. "What is your problem, mate?"

He shrugged. "I just didn't feel like dancing anymore."

Tink and Sydney sat watching quietly through our little altercation.

"You just don't walk off without telling me why. I thought it was something I did."

"Why? I don't owe you any explanations."

"No, you don't. But what you did was just bloody rude. Mates don't do that."

"So, we're mates are we?"

I sighed. "I thought we were." I stood up and stormed off. Queens. Sometimes they're worse than women. Okay, you can call my attitude what you like – and you're probably right – but if Muscles was angry or something, why couldn't he just talk it over?

Muttering to myself, determined to get off the island as soon as I could, I felt someone grab my arm and spin me around. I felt a little thrill that Muscles had followed me, but that was supplanted by total shock when he pulled me to him, planting his lips on mine, pushing his tongue into my mouth. I was so taken by surprise that I reacted by starting to tongue tussle with him. He kissed like a dream and it did things to my body. I wasn't thinking straight at that moment, only later did I excuse my reaction it on the grounds that I missed Tina.

Our kisses were so ravenous I thought we were in danger of devouring each other's face. When we broke for air, it hit me hard that I'd just snogged another dude, that I'd enjoyed it, and that I'd felt his hard-on pressing into my groin. What totally threw me was that I was as hard as he was. I couldn't cope with that. I ran for it. I ran as fast and as far as I could, until I reached the sandy beach, deserted except for a few couples making out in the sand. My head was in turmoil. I watched the couples for a while, even the one actually fucking in the sand. I wondered what it was that made it so different in my mind to me and Tina doing the same thing. I missed her so much.

That was no excuse for what Muscles did, or what I did in return. What the fuck is wrong with me? Sure, I like Muscles, but only as a mate. You don't go around shoving your tongue down your mate's throat, unless it's a joke to gross him out. I don't think that's what Muscles was trying to do. And, if I thought about it, which I was trying extra hard not to do, then it didn't gross me out. In fact, I really liked the way Muscles kissed: it was tough but tender, not the insipid mouth open tolerance Tina seemed to present. She was so fuckin' passive half the time like she was waiting for me to get it over and done with.

I stayed out as late as I dared, watching the couple fucking, wondering why the guy who had the cock wedged in his butt was whimpering like he was enjoying every minute. Surely, it hurt like fuck? As I walked back to the bungalow, passing couples and threesomes, plus a few unknowns off in the bushes, I hoped Muscles was in bed. I really didn't want to talk about what happened tonight. I didn't want to talk about it ever.

The light was on when I got back. Damn. I let myself in, intending to head straight to my bedroom avoiding any sort of conversation. As I closed the door, I saw Muscles seated on the lounge watching some shit on the flat screen. Without looking up, he muttered, "Sorry," and that was that. End of discussion. I went to bed and by the time I woke up the next morning, everything was back to normal.

I'd made no friends on the island, apart from Muscles, and I desperately needed someone to talk to. I made an appointment to see Trent Franklin.

"Not enjoying it here, Mr. Cody?" he asked when I asked how his search for a replacement was going.

"Slight complication," I responded.

"Your bungalow share coming on too strong for your liking?"

"No, Yes. No," I fudged. "Look, as long as this goes no further…"

"You have my word."

"We were getting along great but, last night...last night, he kissed me."

Franklin anticipated. "And you liked it? You got hard? And now you're very confused?"

"That's about it," I admitted.

"Mr. Cody, there's a reason we don't employ straight men on this island. And what you're experiencing now is the reason. I was hoping you would turn out differently because there is nothing but praise for your work here. You are an asset to Rainbow Cove now that you've settled in. I'd even singled you out for a special assignment when you come back from your well-earned leave. I take it you are going back to the mainland in search of pussy to re-establish your heterosexual credentials?"

"That was the intention."

"After you come back we have a very special client staying with us. Very hush hush because...well, you'll understand why when I tell you who it is. This is in the strictest confidence, Mr. Cody, but we will be playing host to Jason Gianfranco while he films his latest movie on the Sunshine Coast."

"Holy fuck, Gianfranco is gay?"

"Now you can see why it's of the utmost importance to keep it quiet. If newspapers ever got wind of it..."

I wanted to rush back and tell Muscles. He'd be over the moon.

"Why me?"

"You just seemed the perfect fit. He needs swimming and scuba diving lessons while he's here. You have the qualifications. He lied to the studio about his aquatic expertise so he doesn't want to be found out. It will be our little secret. Do you think you're up for the challenge?"

"Shit, yeah."

"That's what I like to hear. Now, if you'll excuse me…"

I was dismissed. As I walked back to the cabin to tell Muscles the news, I realized I'd been the victim of a snow job. Franklin had essentially bribed me into staying on. I knew one thing for sure, I really did need Muscles to help me get an entirely new wardrobe of clothes. I couldn't be seen with Jason Gianfranco in flip flops.

Muscles was pissed that the straight guy was getting to be up close and personal with his favorite action star and not him. "He'll probably use the gym to keep fit, especially if he's in the middle of making a movie. He'll want to look his best."

"They give all the VIPs to Leon because this is his third year here. It's a reward for his loyalty."

"Maybe I could put in a good word for you. Invite him over for supper, or to watch TV, and you can impress him with your big muscle."

He laughed. "Don't be dirty."

I breathed easier, it looked as if we'd both put the previous night back in the box.

"Are you still up for taking me shopping? Otherwise I'll come back with nothing but shit."

In the end, it cost an absolute fortune, depleting a lot of the cash I'd put away for my reunion with Tina. I confided in Muscles about my plan to pursue her to Europe and present her with an engagement ring. I think he was sincere when he said that was really romantic, then added, "She won't recognize you in your new clothes. Why don't we post pics of the new you on Facebook? I'll bet she'll be impressed with the makeover."

Every time I took an item of clothing off the rack to try on, Muscles would quietly return it, instead handing me a pile of stuff I never would have considered once. I was taken aback when he came into the dressing room with me but it was only to get me set up, then he went outside to wait with the cute female shop assistant who thought we were a couple because we were at Rainbow Cove. I heard Muscles telling her my life story, pimping me out to this hot chick. I owed him big time for that.

He could have just let her go on believing I was gay. "He's definitely fuckable," she confided. "Where's he staying while he's on the mainland?"

"He hasn't decided yet," Muscles lied. The resort had three two-bedroom condominiums in one of the top apartment towers overlooking the marina.

"I'm sure my flat mate won't mind if he wants to stay with us," she offered.

Fuckin' ace. I'd get my leg over after all.

I modeled the clothes in various combinations and Muscles was flabbergasted at how well I scrubbed up. As I prepared to parade about in the next set of clothes, I called from the changing booth, "I need some help here." I had my fingers crossed that Muscles was astute enough to send Cherie, the shop assistant. Good man, he did. He also covered for us while she was down on her knees blowing me until I dumped a load in her throat. She grimaced as if it tasted bad. Still it was hot to watch my cock disappear into a chick's mouth again even if she choked on it. I wondered whether Muscles could take it all without gagging. I was willing to bet that he could.

After I'd paid for the purchases, I took Muscles for a meal in thanks for helping me out. My choice of a Thai restaurant, because we both like Thai food, turned out to be inspired because the waiter took a shine to Muscles who was just as impressed with him. I should have been happy because it was obvious these two were gonna consummate their attraction about the same time I was feeding my cock to Cherie. Then why the hell did I feel a twitch of…what was it? Envy? Jealousy? Nah, I was glad my mate was gonna get his knob polished. What was left unsaid was…I wished it was me with Muscles.

Thank god, Cherie and her flat mate took my mind off my severe lapse of heteroness. I left Muscles talking to the Thai boy wondering why, if I was his type, he was talking to a slim pretty boy the antithesis of me.

To fill in time until Cherie finished work, I went to the movies. Can't even remember what I watched because I was so used to having Muscles share with me. We both had a similar sense of humor and he got my stupid jokes. I tried to get my mind on Cherie and her as yet unseen flat mate. Maybe she was as hot as Cherie and they'd put on a double act for me and then I could join in. Or maybe, I could sneak into her room after I'd fucked Cherie.

Muscles was taking my clothes with him when he returned to Rainbow Cove on the cat the next day while I had four remaining days of freedom. In the end, I didn't last the distance. I doubt I would have even without the shock. Cherie was an accomplished lover but she wanted me to eat her out for hours on end. Look, I love eating pussy as much as I love eating McDonalds, which is a lot, but she had me down between her thighs until my face and tongue threatened to seize up. She was more concerned with her own pleasure; mine was an afterthought, and then she helped out only reluctantly.

Her flat mate turned on me because, I suspect, she wanted to be the one between Cherie's legs. Good luck to her. By day three I was ready to call it quits. Left alone in their small one-bedroom flat while they were both at work, I was going insane with boredom. I'd tried unsuccessfully to contact Tina. I'd even uploaded the rather flattering pics of me in my new outfits on Facebook. I thought Tina may have seen them and at least clicked Like. Nothing but silence.

She hadn't updated her own Facebook page for a while so I wasn't expecting anything different that day. When I went to check, she'd unfriended me, and I couldn't access her page at all. WTF? I don't know what made me decide to check my brother's page. After an initial curiosity about what he was up to early in my stay at Rainbow Cove, I hadn't bothered checking again, assuming he was hard at work on his uni stuff. I'd been very misguided. I scrolled down the page. Almost six weeks ago it began with "I'm in Europe and guess who I ran into in Paris, the City of Love?" There was a photo of Rhett and Tina looking much too pleased to be in each other's company. There were almost hourly updates on where they were, what they'd had for lunch/dinner/breakfast, how they wished their friends could be with them, how much they enjoyed each other's company.

It all smacked of a set-up. They very quickly admitted that in a city such as Paris it was inevitable that they'd fall in love. Bullshit! Now that I looked back on it, Tina had been withdrawn in the last few months we'd been together. She'd obviously been seeing Rhett behind my back. I bet her cunt of a father had set the whole thing up. I scrolled through the more recent protestations of true love and how fortuitous their meeting had been. I guessed they'd been on the same plane together and that Tina's dad had paid for the ticket.

I came across an upload that was less than five minutes old. "I just asked Tina to marry me…"

I slammed my phone down in a temper, not wanting to read any more. I had to concentrate on my breathing. I was gutted. The enormity of what Tina and my brother had done to me took my breath away. I'd be a laughing stock among all our friends, although I guess they'd all be Tina and Rhett's friends now. Shit, how could I ever show my face in the city again? I needed to breathe. I needed to talk to someone. I couldn't wait until Cherie got home, besides, I doubted she'd care. I had to get back to the island. Trent Franklin would listen. He was good at advising people what to do. He'd know what brand of high-powered rifle or which poison would be most effective in dispatching Tina and her obnoxious father, as well as my treacherous brother, in the most painful manner.

Glancing at my watch, I saw I had thirty minutes to get to the marina if I wanted to catch the catamaran back to Rainbow Cove. I could probably hold it together until I got back. I had to because there were bound to be guests on the boat with me and the last thing they'd want to see is one of the staff having a total breakdown.

I grabbed my backpack, stuffing the few items I'd brought over with me, glad now that Muscles had persuaded me to bring a pair of running shoes to complement my flip flops. I wrote on the kitchen whiteboard a big thank you and a short explanation to the girls for my sudden disappearance, slammed their flat door behind me, and scrambled down three flights of stairs to the street.

I had little idea where I was so I hailed a cab and told the driver he'd get double fare if he got me to my destination in time. He put his foot down, barely missing a number of jaywalking pedestrians who assumed the laid-back coastal city style also applied to their taxi drivers. Not this one. He got me to the wharf in record time. I threw a handful of notes at him and made a dash for the cat which was ready to cast off. I screamed for them to wait. They must have heard because they stopped until I ran up gasping for breath. One of the crew helped me aboard and I slumped in a molded plastic seat to catch my breath. The guests, fortunately, were on the upper deck where the seats were leather and the aperitifs plentiful.

The journey seemed to take forever and I only just kept my emotional breakdown at bay by fanning my anger. That worked only so long. When I knew I was about to lose it totally I took a chance and pressed Muscles' cell phone number. If he was busy he wouldn't answer. God, I needed him to. Someone must have heard my prayer because he picked up.

"Hey, Ty, how's it going, mate? You enjoying your pussy break."

I blubbered. I confess it, I just blubbered down the phone. I know I made no sense but Muscles let me get it out before he took charge. "Hold on, mate. Take a deep breath." He got my breathing sorted out and then talked me through to calmness. I was borderline okay. He told me he'd head to the wharf to meet me and then I could tell him all about it. "No matter how bad it is, mate, we can lick it. You'll be all right, you'll see." By the time he disconnected, I was starting to believe him. I'd never felt so bad in my entire life before.

The trip seemed to take an eternity. When we docked at the wharf, as a staff member I was supposed to allow the guests to disembark first. Fuck that, my needs were more immediate. I jumped the gap before the crew had even tied up, narrowly avoiding injury. Curses followed as I ran down the jetty toward Muscles who had somehow commandeered a golf buggy. Suddenly it seemed like the nicest thing anyone had ever done for me. Flinging myself onto the seat next to him, Muscles took off without asking unnecessary questions. There'd be time for the third-degree later. I kept the sobs at bay but the tears were falling. I guess I owed at least a perfunctory explanation for my unusual behavior. I managed to say, "She's marrying my fuckin' brother."

Muscles put his arm around my shoulder to pull me closer. I rested my head against him and felt better already. We soon reached our bungalow and he helped me inside where I collapsed against his massive chest and just let it all out. I know I wasn't making any sense as I railed against their treachery and how I was going to disembowel Tina's old man who I saw as responsible for the whole debacle. I slowly ran out of steam until I was just venting. I assumed Muscles got the gist of what I was saying although all he did was hold me until it was time to shut me up. He kissed me. Hard. On the mouth. Taking me by surprise. But it was so warm and wonderful, I kissed him back. He was so comfortable. I don't know what I would have done if it hadn't been for him.

"I think you should lie down," he said softly as he pushed me toward my bedroom.

"Don't take this the wrong way, but I don't want to be alone tonight."

He steered me toward his bedroom. He'd decorated it, making it distinctly his whereas my room still had the air of a motel about it. He lit two candles beside the bed, their flicker calming me further. He undressed me even as I attempted to kiss him again. Eventually, he pushed me back on the bed so he could drag my trousers off. I was naked apart from my briefs. I reached up and pulled him down on top of me, tearing at his shirt because I wanted to feel his skin against mine. After I lifted his top over his head because I was too impatient to undo the buttons, I attacked his shorts. I had them unzipped and down around his knees before he could stop me. He kicked them off.

We were skin to skin, cock to cock although they were still snuggled behind the cotton of our briefs. I ran my hands over the smooth skin of his back, tanned to perfection. He ran his fingers across the light fuzz on my chest, tweaking my nipples as he passed, making me buck each time he squeezed. It must have given him the idea to paste his lips around each nub in turn, nipping slightly until I thought my cock would explode.

Slipping my hand under the waist band of his briefs, I squeezed his muscular butt cheeks, wishing I had the nerve to explore his warm crevice and his hot, tight hole. My brain kept telling me that I wasn't gay, but my cock didn't agree, especially when Muscles slid down the bed, dragging my briefs over my cock so it sprang free and proud. He rubbed the tip with his thumb, smearing my pre-cum around the head. I jumped because it felt so sensitive.

He nuzzled my balls with his nose before I felt his tongue lap my scrotum. No one had ever done that to me before. He held my shaft perpendicular in order to lick up the underside until he reached the ridge that was the head of my prick. His tongue felt so good. I wanted to feel his cock but it was out of reach so I had to content myself with stroking his hair. He was so tender I thought I'd blow my wad at any moment but he knew what he was doing, bringing me to a peak and then backing off. It was exquisite torture.

He moved back up my body, obviously having removed his own briefs at some stage while he was licking my cock. Now we were totally naked, grinding against each other in a wild effort to reach climax. I didn't want it to end like this. "Fuck me. Please."

"Are you sure?" he whispered.

I nodded my consent.

He slid back down the bed, engulfing my entire cock in his mouth until I slid painlessly into his throat. I was right, he didn't gag. I don't know why that made me feel so proud of him. I wanted him to fuck me but instead he was about to drain my balls with his very expert oral technique. I wanted to complain but I simply couldn't; he was too good. I lay back and let him do what he did best – siphon all the spunk out of my balls. I writhed on the bed, forcing my cock as far down his throat as I could manage, holding the back of his head for leverage. He took all the punishment I meted out and came back for more.

I warned him I was about to come in case he was like Tina and hated the taste in his mouth. No, he took it all, first in his throat and later on his tongue, sucking to get every last drop until the head was so sensitive I couldn't take any more. He crawled up on top of me again and placed his lips against mine. I hesitated for a split second before opening up to taste myself in his mouth. It wasn't unpleasant and to show I wasn't at all repulsed I sucked his tongue until I was afraid I'd pull it out by the root.

"You nice and relaxed?" he asked.

"Mm," I responded sleepily.

Muscles licked his way down my body, via my nipples, my biceps, my abs, my dick, my balls, until he reached that line that leads to your asshole. Suddenly he lifted my legs in the air, asking me to pull them back against my chest as far as I could. I was bent almost double but it gave him access to my ass. He bent down to run his tongue against my vulnerable hole. I shivered, not quite sure I was ready for this now. "Relax," he said. "You'll love it."

I tried, but as soon as his tongue touched my sphincter, it closed up, threatening to never open again. He slapped my butt cheek enough to hurt and I must have relaxed a little because the next thing I knew he was inserting his tongue into my butt hole. It felt so good, I wanted to hold his face there forever, but I knew this was only foreplay for what I'd begged him to do earlier. There was no backing out now, even if I wanted to.

He chewed, licked, and tongue-fucked my ass until I was whimpering before he reached into the drawer on the bedside table to retrieve a tube of lube and a strip of condoms. He tore the foil with his teeth and sheathed his cock. Then he squirted a liberal amount of gel against my asshole, working it in with his fingers until he had three buried inside me. He rubbed the excess lube over the condom before he pushed his cock against my entrance. I seized up in panic, making it impossible for him to breach my hole. What had I been thinking when I begged him to fuck me?

He leaned down to nibble on my chest again, clamping his teeth over my left nipple and biting down hard. I screamed in pain and he slid his cock into the folds of my anus, breaching me. "You asshole," I grinned, somewhere between pleasure and pain.

"Nah, I think it's your asshole wrapped around my cock."

He kissed me and, as I responded, he slipped his cock farther into my guts. I'd like to say it didn't hurt, but it did. Okay, it burned rather than hurt. Until it hit something inside me that almost had me clinging to the ceiling. "What the fuck was that?"

"Ah, I found it. Now, just lie back and let me show you what it's all about."

I didn't believe him for a moment, but after he'd pushed his substantial cock against whatever it was in my butt, making my prick sit up and take notice again, I'd have to rethink my predicament. Somewhere in the near future I would also have to calculate whether I was giving myself to Muscles because I wanted to, as a reward for his kindness, or because I was trying to get back at Tina. Or a combination of all three. Just for the moment, however, I would allow myself to wallow in some of the best sex I'd ever had in my life.

He picked up the pace, fucking me hard, making me grunt every time he hit that button inside me which, in turn, forced drools of cum from my dick slit. I wanted to jerk my cock but Muscles replaced my hand with his own, milking me steadily in tune with the thrusts into my ass. I was about to tell him I couldn't hold off much longer when he whispered, "Come for me, baby" as he gave a superhuman thrust, gritted his teeth, made a series of noises and obviously shot his load inside me, while I was busy groaning as I shot my wad onto my belly and chest.

Once we'd both regained our breath, he pulled out slowly, holding the condom in place so it wouldn't slip off. He tied the end and disposed of it in a bin beside the bed, lowering my legs so I could stretch to get rid of the slight cramp. He grabbed a handful of tissues from a box on the nightstand to wipe me clean, then pulled the sheet over our naked bodies, kissing me once again before asking, "I hope you don't regret what we just did?"

"Hell, no. I just hope I was okay."

"Better than okay. You have no idea how long I've wanted to do that."

"I'm beginning to get an idea."

I would have been up for a longer discussion but the trauma of the day, and having come twice in the throes of great sex, sent me to sleep in record time. I only awoke because someone had their very special and very warm mouth around my prick as the sun shone through the bedroom window.

"Morning, Muscles," I said cheerily as I lifted the sheet to watch him take my cock all the way into his gullet. He was too polite to answer. Caressing his head as he took care of my morning woody, I wondered how my brain was going to react to all this once it had caught up with my body. At least the next two days I was on vacation so I'd have the time to work through the turmoil in my life. The one thing I knew for sure was that I wouldn't be flying to Paris to try to tempt Tina back. I knew I'd lost that battle. Besides, I didn't have the money. My most major concern was whether sex with Muscles meant I was gay. Or bisexual? Or merely curious?

Muscles must have heard the gears inside my head attempting to come to terms with my actions. "Stop thinking about it. It'll work itself out in the end."

I tried for levity. "If you swallow my junk, does that mean we're gay engaged?"

He gagged on my cock because he was trying not to laugh. Wiping the drool from his lips, he replied, "That's entirely up to you. But whatever you decide, whether it's a one-off, or you want to do it again either with or without me, though I hope it is with me, don't ever feel guilty about what we did."

My guilt DNA hadn't kicked in as yet. I hoped it wouldn't.

I blew down his throat as he jerked off on the sheets.

The next two days I spent licking my metaphorical wounds. Muscles caught me at my laptop writing abuse which I was about to plant on Rhett's Facebook page. He grabbed my hand, deleting my diatribe before I could send it. Instead, I unfriended my own brother. His last posting was about their nuptials in Paris in a month's time. I mentally wished them both hideous deaths, mentally closing the door on that part of my life. I felt freer than I had in quite a while, although I was afraid that I had yet to find myself again. Tina had been so much a part of my life and my plans that I wasn't sure I had a purpose any more.

I guess Muscles and I became what is known as secret fuck buddies. We spent every waking moment together, far more intimate in our behavior as we watched movies together, usually ending up in his bed with a string of condoms on either side. It was the second night before I got to plug his ass. "I don't do this very often, so take it slowly," he said as he lifted his legs in the air. It was too soon for me to consider licking his ass; I didn't even do that to Tina. Mind you, she never allowed me to do anal with her no matter how much I begged. Now that I had time to think about it, Tina actually didn't allow me to do much at all. Muscles was considerably more adventurous. As I pushed my cock into his ass, I wanted to please the man beneath me so badly I realized I would do just about anything for him. All he had to do was snap his fingers and I'd be there.

But he made no demands. I appreciated the freedom he gave me because the last thing I wanted at that moment was to make a commitment. I don't mean to Muscles, I mean to which side of the sexual fence my loyalties lay, or whether I was straddling that same fence. Time for that later, though I wondered why I'd ever have to make that decision. Was I gay or just gay for Muscles? As I went about my duties at the pool and on the beach, it gave me the opportunity to stare at almost naked hot men. Yeah, some of them I marked down as guys I'd fuck, some that I'd let fuck me, more I'd let gnaw on my cock. While I was daydreaming, my cock was thickening in my Speedos. Yeah, I was at least a little bit gay. Or maybe I was just sexual.

I even began to experiment with sucking cock. Muscles was patient, even when my teeth scraped painfully against his knob. He taught me how to control my breathing when I had his cock in my mouth, how to sheath my teeth, all the little secrets that add up to good oral technique. We also began to watch some of the porn on the cable channels piped through to the bungalow. We started with bi porn but soon moved on to totally gay. It was an entirely new world to me. I loved the way men could take their pleasure in a strong, masculine way. Tina was always moaning that it hurt, or not to fuck her so hard. Okay, she was probably an exception but the prissy way Cherie treated my cum didn't endear her to me either. Maybe it was me. The first time Muscles shot in my mouth, I thought I'd die. I couldn't swallow it, so he sucked it into his own gob and swallowed before kissing me to let me get used to the residual taste.

Slowly, I got accustomed to swallowing.

A lot of guys noticed the change in me, most of them putting it down to the fact I'd got my share of pussy on the mainland. I put up with a number of sarcastic jibes, until I overheard a group of what I called 'queens' discussing me. They didn't know I could hear them.

"I bet he's not straight," one of them hissed.

I still hadn't revealed that I'd sort of changed teams to anyone at the resort. It was a secret between me and Muscles. As far as I knew he hadn't even spilled the beans to Tink whose relationship with Sydney was now well-established. I wondered if a relationship was what I wanted with Muscles.

"Of course, he's straight. That girl in the menswear store on the mainland said he fucked her silly all during his vacation time."

"Methinks he was trying to prove something to himself."

"Maybe he's bi."

"As in bi bi heterosexuality?"

The group laughed.

"You're just bitter because you lost the bet."

What bet?

"The odds are it'll be that actor, Gianfranco who's arriving next week. I bet he'll convert our so-called straight boy."

"Well, whoever it is, they stand to make a lot of money from all the bets that have been placed so far."

"You think he has any idea how much his cherry ass is worth to the guy who fucks him first."

"I just wish it was me. I'd do him for free."

"You're a bottom, Simon. He'd be doing you."

"Even better money if that person can make him fall in love with them."

I was stunned for a moment. People were taking bets on who'd turn me gay? WTF? I thought all this time that Muscles liked me. He sure did a great impersonation of someone who had feelings. Just as well I hadn't voiced my own. Those emotions I did have had just shriveled up into a small sick knot in my stomach.

I barely got through the day. If what Tina and Rhett had done was a major betrayal, then Muscles deserved the very worst that I could visit on him. I thanked whoever was looking after me that I'd got the warning in time.

Storming back to the bungalow after my shift, I sat and seethed until I heard Muscles come in. He didn't notice the look of thunder on my face otherwise he would not have come near me. He kissed the top of my head as usual, "How was your day, babe?"

I gritted my teeth to prevent myself from growling. "I learned something really interesting today. You may not find it as absorbing as I did, but then you knew about it already. In fact, you're part of it. You must have really been laughing at me behind my back. How many people know you've been fucking me?"

"I haven't told anyone."

"How do you expect to win the bet then?"

I heard his sharp intake of breath. "How did you find out about that?"

"A group of queens who couldn't keep their mouths shut. I overheard them."

"Stupid buggers."

"So, it's true?"

"There's nothing to it, Ty. No one is going to claim the prize."

"Why's that?"

"Because I am never going to tell them."

"Is that because you were waiting for me to tell you that I love you?"

"No, for god's sake…what?"

"Where's your phone?"

He pulled it out of his pocket. I grabbed it, turning it on the two of us, and said straight to camera. "Yeah, it's me, the straight boy. You can all collect on your bets now because this man standing right beside me fucked me in the ass when I was at my most vulnerable. Took my cherry ass. Was so good at his task, I got to like the way his cock felt inside me. He even managed to wangle his way into my heart. I was all set to tell him that I had feelings for him. Yeah, you heard that right. I genuinely liked this guy. It's obvious he's hot. Good looks, good body, and for those who haven't experienced it yet, a dick to die for. And he knows how to use it."

Muscles struggled to get out of my grip but I wouldn't let him go.

"But it's what's on the inside that counts. He's kind, he's caring, he's smart, he's funny. I could go on all day, but I found out it was all an act. I found out he's just doing it for the money. So, I'm making this video to put you all out of your misery and you can pay him what's he owed."

I switched the video recorder off and slammed the phone back in Muscles' hand. Banging the front door on my way out gave me immense satisfaction even though it was a childish act. I couldn't believe that after knowing him such a short time that Muscles' betrayal hurt much more than Tina's. What the fuck was wrong with me that everyone ends up screwing me over?

I headed for the beach, my usual spot to get a bit of perspective in my life. I avoided the lovers and the groups, finding myself a secluded area on the edge of the rocks. I gazed out to sea, lulled by the gentle swell of the ocean, wondering what other horrors lay in store for me.

Time passed and the beach lovers ebbed and flowed like the waves breaking on the shore. I don't know how long I sat there but the moon was high in the sky when I heard someone behind me. If anyone put the hard word on me tonight I was likely to snap their head off.

"Did you mean what you said back in the bungalow," the voice asked softly.

"Which part?"

"About having feelings for me?"

I sighed. "What does it matter now?"

"Ty, I've loved you from the moment I met you. Stupid, I know. I almost went insane having you as my room-mate. So many times I wanted to request a move but you always did something that endeared you to me even more and I just had to stay. When you gave yourself to me that night you found out that Tina was going to marry your brother, I hoped, I prayed, it wasn't just for once. When it continued, I couldn't believe my luck."

He bowed his head against mine, but I refused to look at him.

"I love you so much, Ty. It's not easy for a big guy like me to say those words. And I've never said them to another man ever. I'm sorry I hurt you. I should have told you about the stupid bet before this. I was never part of it. Oh, I don't expect you to believe that, but it's true."

I did believe him even though I didn't want to. I wanted to stay angry because he hadn't told me.

"I'm so pissed off with you," I said, although my voice belied my words. "You should have told me."

"I didn't want you to think for even one minute that what I felt for you had anything to do with that stupid wager."

He sniffed, and my heart broke. "Aw, shit, now you've got me all tearful," I sobbed.

Our heads were still together as we both snuffled, wiping our nose on the backs of our hand.

"Come back, Ty. Let me make it up to you. I'll never tell anyone about us, not until you say it's all right."

I put my arm around him, pulling him in to lick his salty tears away. "Give me a little time to forgive you. I will eventually, because I love you, Muscles. There, I said it. You win the bet. How much was the pot?"

Muscles quoted a figure in the thousands. I whistled. "That would make a pretty start to our married life."

"What?"

I sank to my knees in front of him. "Muscles, will you do me the honor of marrying me?"

He sank down beside me. "Fuck, yeah."

We kissed until our lips were raw, then we helped each other up and went back to the bungalow arm in arm. I broke away from his grip whenever we passed other couples. He thought I was still coming to terms with our relationship.

Once we were home, we consummated our feelings for each other – twice. In the afterglow as I lay staring at the darkened ceiling, I asked, "How much did you say the prize was worth?"

He repeated the figure.

"Gianfranco is here next week. People are betting he's the one who'll bust my cherry, which should make your odds…"

"What are you thinking?"

"We should use these guys at their own game. Wait until Gianfranco leaves—"

"You think you'll be able to resist his charms."

"He's not my type. You are."

"Are you suggesting we scam the bastards?"

"Yep. Once the movie star leaves, we can make the big announcement that you fucked me so hard you turned me gay and that I fell in love with your dick."

He laughed. "We wouldn't exactly be lying, would we?"

"Except that I fell in love with all of you."

"What would we do with the money?"

I thought about it. "How about we take a holiday and return to work again at Rainbow Cove next summer? I like it here. I'll like it even more as a gay man."

"Where would you like to go for this vacation of ours?"

"I hear Paris is beautiful in April."

LOVE WITH A SIDE ORDER OF PELICANS

"But, daddy, you promised."

I knew I was a lousy dad. I didn't need my young daughter, Penny, whining in my ear to confirm it. Is there anything more irritating than the unreasonable demands of a five-year-old reminding you of your non-existent parenting skills? Kids have no concept of adult responsibilities. They don't demand equal time with making a living, doing the laundry, buying the groceries; they want one hundred and ten per cent of your attention and they want it now.

In case I missed her accusation, Penny pouted, folding her arms tightly against her chest as she always does when she's not getting her way. On this occasion, it wasn't my fault. That made not one iota of difference.

"Honey, daddy can't help it if the traffic is bad."

Reality and reasonableness had no effect. "You promised."

I looked on the dashboard for the button that would eject Penny's child restraint car seat through the roof and way out into space so I could no longer hear her whining. If I was completely honest, it was my fault we were running late. I had to answer a few more important emails; more important than my daughter's happiness. That's how we got stuck in the traffic attempting to escape the city on a Saturday morning along with loads of other weekenders.

What's a dad to do in a situation like that? I lied.

"Honey, we'll make it. They never start on time. If they do, we'll be there a few minutes after they begin the feeding."

Not unreasonably, Penny retorted, "I want a seat at the front, not behind a whole lot of gown-ups who block my view. You promised, daddy."

I checked my watch again. No way were we going to get to our destination a few minutes after the show had begun. We'd be lucky to get there before it ended. Penny gave me the cold shoulder for the remainder of the trip, the atmosphere in the vehicle icy.

I couldn't expect a child to understand the economics. I ran my own single-employee business, my income precarious at the best of times, especially if I didn't work. Even though I'd promised the weekend would be totally devoted to her enjoyment, I'd intended to spend the early morning on my computer, catching up on important work while she slept. But she hadn't slept. She was up and ready to leave while I was still in the middle of a job so important I couldn't shut down the computer.

Kids cost money. For a start, Penny was forever growing out of clothes, and that was only if they lasted into obsolescence as she gave everything a thorough work-out. She could easily have a career as a tester for children's fashions. If she was hard on her clothes, she was doubly trying on my nerves. She'd gone from badgering me with her questions and demands about how long the trip was taking, through pouting, to glancing at her plastic watch every few minutes and sighing deeply.

I needed something to bribe her. "I'll buy you an ice cream when we get to the beach," I said, hoping her love of ice cream would overcome her disappointment. Wrong!

"Oh, daddy. You really think an ice cream will make up for it if we miss the pelicans?"

"You're right. We'll have fish and chips on the beach."

She shook her little head as if her father was a major disappointment and had no idea of the importance of getting to watch the pelicans feed. She seethed with irritation; refusing to look at me, concentrating her energies on gazing out the window.

By the time I'd found a spot in the coastal town's free car park after driving around and around until a shopper, laden with supermarket goods, vacated, and then found our way out of the labyrinthine five-story nightmare of abandoned shopping trolleys and angry motorists, we got to the lake as the last stragglers were leaving the designated pelican feeding zone. It was a brick and concrete amphitheater with the water at the mouth so the pelicans could waddle on shore to be fed while the audience sat on the brick semi-circular raised levels.

"See, daddy," Penny shrieked. "I told you we'd be late."

Even though I mentally blamed the traffic, my job, my timing, even my lousy luck, I knew deep down we should have left earlier, taken no chances on all the variables that can turn a pleasure to a disaster. I had a headache just thinking about it.

"It's all your fault," Penny screamed.

People turned to stare at the little girl flinging accusations at her father.

"Please, honey, we'll come back tomorrow."

My attempts to placate fell on deaf ears. There's no reasoning with a child who has a one-track desire.

She did stamp her foot this time. "I don't want to come back tomorrow. I want to see the pelicans now!"

"Look. There are plenty of pelicans swimming in the lake and, see, there are a couple of them sleeping on the sandbank."

She wasn't to be appeased. "They're too far away. I want to pet one."

"I don't know whether you're allowed to touch them," I said.

She'd brook no argument. "Of course, you are."

When Little Miss Know-it-all gets on her high horse, there's no arguing with her. She sat down on the brickwork, a grimace of determination on her face.

"What are you doing, Penny?"

"I'm getting a good seat for tomorrow."

"You can't sit there all night."

"Yes, I can."

I sat down beside her, noticing for the first time the young man who was cleaning up the garbage obviously left by the crowds who'd watched the pelican feeding earlier. He seemed a little too interested in the confrontation between Penny and me. The hide of the man. I was about to tell him off when I realized he had just as much right to be here as we did; perhaps more right.

"When I said 'tomorrow' I didn't actually mean tomorrow, Penny. Daddy has important work he has to finish and we need to go back to town. I'll see if I can squeeze a day off next weekend. How's that?"

Penny looked at me as if I had just crushed all respect for adults out of her. There were no tantrums, no screaming this time. She just spoke with deadly calm. "You said tomorrow."

I knew defeat when I heard it. There was no wriggle room left.

"I'll have to see if we can find a hotel for the night. Daddy doesn't have a lot of money for extras like that. It would be better if we could come back next week."

Penny was through negotiating. "Tomorrow."

I glared at the council cleaner leaning on his pick-up claw watching our drama unfold. I hoped the look on my face reminded him to mind his own business and leave us alone. It obviously didn't work as he strolled casually in our direction. When he was about three meters away, he stopped, pretending to collect rubbish in his vicinity but merely snapping at thin air with the claw on the end of a wooden rod.

He looked at us more closely, before he said, "So, you want to see a pelican?"

From the look of excitement on Penny's face, I could see how easily children could be lured away. I'd warned her repeatedly about strangers. I hoped it was because I was with her that she'd lowered her stranger danger faculties.

"I have a pelican," he continued.

It might have been the murderous look on my face, for he backed off a little. He opened the trash bag he had attached to his belt and after scrounging through it for a few moments, extracted a crumpled leaflet. He tossed it toward me.

I left it on the ground where it fell.

"Read it," he suggested.

I leaned forward to pick it up, my eyes never leaving him. Smoothing it out carefully, I saw that it was a leaflet for the pelican feeding, giving a brief history of the area and how the public feeding came about as a tourist attraction. The flip side had a large illustration of a pelican with bullet points about their life cycle. Penny looked at the leaflet with interest. I raised my eyes to the interloper.

"The side that gives the history of the feeding."

I turned the brochure back over.

Penny saw it before I did. She poked her finger at the photograph in the bottom right-hand corner.

"That's you," she exclaimed excitedly. "You feed the pelicans."

"Yup," he said simply.

She thrust the leaflet into my hands. "Daddy, that's the man who feeds the pelicans."

I had to restrain her from running over to him.

"What have I told you about strangers?"

Penny had her own logic. She reiterated, "He's not a stranger, daddy. He's the man who feeds the pelicans."

The guy came closer, squatting in front of Penny so he was more at her level.

"You must be Penny," he said, in a voice so smooth she was instantly smitten. It probably had the same effect on women.

"He knows my name, daddy," she said, pleased as punch. Of course, he did. He'd heard us arguing earlier. I had to give him credit, though; he'd got her out of the funk that had threatened our entire visit.

"What's your name?" she asked.

"You can call me Spike." He held his hand out for Penny to shake which, I knew from experience, makes her feel very grown up.

Then Spike turned his attention to me. There was something about him. Perhaps it was his eyes that were as greeny blue as the water in the lake. Or maybe the smile. I couldn't work it out but he had a quality about him that drew you in, made you like him, made you feel important.

"And what do I call daddy?"

I stood suddenly to break the spell, wiping my hands on the legs of my trousers to dislodge the sand, before offering to shake his hand. "Travis Black."

His grip was strong and friendly. I had a couple of centimeters in height on him, but his arms were thick with muscle, flexing beneath his navy form-hugging official Pelican Feeder button-up shirt. If he was single, he would have women lining up around the block. Not that I was examining him in forensic detail, it was just the conclusion I came to in those seconds a guy sizes up the competition when he first meets another male.

Penny tugged at my hand, anxious about being ignored. Her whine drew our attention back to her.

"So, Penny," Spike said. "About the pelicans."

"We missed them because daddy was busy at his silly old work," she pouted.

"You like to eat, don't you?" Spike asked.

"Of course," she replied.

"Well, your daddy has to work so he can make money in order to buy you food."

The argument didn't seem to convince her. Besides, she had a much better idea.

"Why don't I move in with you, and you can feed me like the pelicans? That way, daddy can spend as much time as he likes at his stupid work."

Spike raised a quizzical brow at me.

"Little girls require a lot of money. I run my own business and, hey, there's a financial squeeze on." I cursed myself for feeling that I had to explain my life to this stranger.

"Blah blah blah," Penny said, not for the first time. I'd attempted to explain why I needed to work rather than drop everything for one of her whims. Our trip today was a treat for all the times I hadn't been able to give her the attention she deserved. Spike's look insinuated there was no excuse for ignoring my daughter.

"How would you like to meet a very special pelican?"

"Can I pat him?" Penny asked eagerly.

"As long as you're very gentle."

"Can I, daddy? Can I?"

I shrugged, feeling as if I were extraneous to the conversation. "That's up to Mr. Donovan."

"Spike."

"Okay. Spike." I really wasn't feeling in a first-name mood.

"I just have to tidy up the area, and then we'll buy some dinner and head over to my place to see Pontus."

"Who's Pontus?"

"He's the little Pelican I'm nursing back to health."

Penny looked up at me expectantly. "All right, as long as we don't take up too much of Spike's time."

Spike examined me as if I was a miserable bastard, always blocking Penny's enthusiasm. Easy for him, she wasn't his daughter.

"You'll be able to see Pontus much sooner if you help me clean up all the rubbish."

"Good luck, mate," I chuckled. "You're talking to a little girl who won't even tidy her room."

Another pitying look as if to suggest I had no idea how to treat a child, before Spike turned away, Penny trotting alongside him, annoyingly proving me wrong.

Spike wouldn't let her handle the garbage, he had her holding the lip of the rubbish bag open when he wanted to deposit more trash inside, or stamping her foot on the empty aluminum soft drink cans so that he could put them in one of the recycling bins dotted around the area. I was content to remain seated on a bench scrolling through my cell phone for important messages. I didn't realize they'd finished clearing the picnic detritus until the phone was suddenly snatched from my hands and switched off by Spike. "I think daddy needs to take a break from his office." He slipped my phone into my pocket despite my protestations about important business calls. His response was a cool, "Nothing is that important."

I could have put forward a cogent case in my defense but I wasn't about to share personal information with him, least of all the precarious state of my finances. I let it be.

"Daddy, did you know pelicans sometimes live for twenty-five years? That must be as old as nana."

She spouted a few more interesting facts about pelicans that Spike had obviously filled her head with, her earlier hissy fit now totally forgotten.

Spike turned to me. "How about we pick up some fish and chips and we go back to my place so Penny can meet Pontus."

I looked at my watch mainly as a signal that we didn't have a lot of time; it's a good one-and-half to two-hour drive back to the city and I had a lot of calls to make. Penny must have understood my meaning because she pleaded, "Please, daddy. I want to see Pontus."

"I guess it won't hurt for just a little while."

Penny jumped and down, clapping her hands in delight. She hadn't been this excited since we'd first set out on our disastrous adventure. She reached out for my hand as Spike tied up the trash and deposited the bag alongside the public bin where it would be picked up later, I assumed, by the council cleaning crew. We followed the pelican feeder across the picnic plaza toward the main street.

"How did the pelican feeding start?" I knew the question would get Spike talking. I have no small talk and I hoped Spike was loquacious enough for both of us. I was also sure Penny would interrupt with her tuppence worth.

"It goes back almost fifty years," Spike said. As we reached the roadway, Penny reached up with her free hand to take one of Spike's. I couldn't help but be a little jealous. "A fisherman named Hubert Chave used to feed the pelicans after he brought his catch in each morning on his boat. Eventually, he got too old for the life, retired from the sea to open up a fish and chips shop. That was the late 1950s when the town was a tourist mecca. Every afternoon, he'd wander across the road and over to the edge of the lake to feed the birds. It usually attracted a crowd.

"Like all good things, though, Bert got too old to continue even that. Bad ticker, though he still worked behind the counter of his shop. Well, the pelicans must have discovered somehow where he worked and every afternoon about the time he used to feed them, a group of the birds would wade ashore, waddle through the picnic area, cross the street about where we are now, and wander into Bert's Fish & Chips shop expecting to be fed.

"Word got around and people flocked to the town to watch this parade of pelicans. When Bert died, he left some money in his will to keep feeding the birds. When that ran out, the local businesses felt the drop-off in tourism. So they banded together to pay for the feeding, although after a few accidents when the giant birds got run down in the street, it was moved back to the lakeside for safety. A little amphitheater was built and I'm just one in a long line of pelican feeders paid by the businesses you see along the sidewalk here."

By the time he'd finished his story we were at the fish and chip emporium where Spike seemed to be well-known. He put in an order I thought was large enough to feed an army, chatting amiably to the young woman behind the counter. From the way she looked at Spike, you could tell she had it bad. I looked for any signs that he was flirting with her, but he seemed totally oblivious to the effects he had on her.

As she wrapped Spike's order in the white butcher's paper, she saw Penny peering up over the edge of the counter. "And who do we have here?"

"I'm Penny," she said.

The shop assistant picked up one of the chips that had fallen out of the wrapping onto the counter. Ascertaining that it was cool enough, she gave it to Penny.

"Well, Penny, what are you doing today?"

"We're going to Spike's place to see a pelican."

"They missed the feeding," Spike explained.

"Caught in traffic," I added.

"Well, any time you're in town, you pop in and see me. I'll give you the best feed of fish and chips this side of the Pacific Ocean. The name's Debbie."

"Will do, Debbie," I smiled, more at the vanity of her claim than anything else.

"We can head back to my place and eat off proper plates with a proper knife and fork, or we can head back to the picnic table and eat with our fingers. What do you say?"

Penny voted not unexpectedly for "Eat with our fingers," as if she'd never done it before. I marveled at Spike's ability to make the mundane exciting.

Once we'd found a vacant table and ensconced ourselves, the seagulls began circling in search of a free feed, some brash enough to land on the table in an attempt to steal food from the spread in front of us. Penny was delighted which just made me feel more guilty that I had neglected her. She chased after the birds, sending them spiraling into the air to escape her flailing arms and legs. She'd attempt to lure them closer by tossing them a chip she'd broken in two in order that it would cool quickly and not burn their throats. Spike and I watched her carefully from the bench where we shared the meal.

"She's a bundle of energy. She must exhaust you," Spike said.

"I guess I've neglected her of late, what with business the way it is."

"Things not good?"

I have no idea why I was telling him these things, except I suddenly felt incredibly lonely. I'd been so involved in keeping my economic head above water, I'd had no time for a social life and I hadn't missed it. Now that I'd taken a short break…

"To call them 'not good' is the biggest understatement of the decade."

"Ouch."

"Ouch, indeed."

"What about Penny's mum?"

How much did I really want to tell him? What the hell? I'd never see him again after today, so what did it matter?

"She walked out on us."

"Sorry."

"Don't be. She's one of the reasons for the dilemma in which I find myself."

"You don't have to tell me if you would rather not."

I had little pride left. "Makes no difference." I took a deep breath. "Penny's mother was a bigamist. She married me and my money. Loved money more than me while I was making it. She was less happy when we were forced to budget. She was a vain woman. Mind you, she had a lot to be vain about. She also had no intention of curtailing her spending. If I couldn't provide…well, she found someone who could. A lot of someones. She packed my bags and moved me out, sending Penny with me. Only after the bills came in did I discover how much she hadn't cut back on her spending until the credit cards were overdrawn to an alarming degree."

"Does Penny know?"

"No. I was going to tell her that her mother died but I thought that would be too traumatic if she bothered to show up again. So I just explained as best I could that she had found someone she loved more than me and that I wanted her to be happy. I was expecting all sorts of awkward questions but Penny is very mature for her age. She just said, 'Mummy never really loved us, did she? She loved her clothes more.' Penny's pretty well-adjusted considering."

"She's an absolute treasure."

"You got any children of your own?"

"I wish."

"You're not married?"

"Nah, just the sorts of relationships you have when you're young and immature. No one even remotely interesting enough to settle down with."

"But you're looking?"

He moaned theatrically. "Oh, God, how I'm looking."

"Seems to be a smorgasbord of choice from what I've seen around here."

"Trouble is this is a holiday town. People come here looking to relax, looking for a good time. Even when it comes to...you know, it's a holiday relationship; nothing permanent."

"A lot of guys would love that. Sex without responsibility."

"Is that what you like?"

"It's been so long I'm not even sure I know how to do it anymore. Between looking after Penny and trying to salvage the business, it doesn't leave time for much else."

"A good-looking guy like you should have no problems."

"That goes double for you."

Spike laughed. "Listen to us. A mutual admiration society." He suddenly got serious. "I'm not a one-night stand sort of guy."

"Guilty," I said. "Sometimes I'll go that route just for the sheer physical contact or the relief, otherwise I'm with you."

I had no idea where this conversation was going and I think we were both glad when Penny interrupted us. "When are we going to see Pontus?"

It was love at first sight. Penny and Pontus. Sounds like a good name for a rom com except I'm talking girl and bird here. The pelican was smaller than the big birds that muscled their way to the front to be fed as a public spectacle. "He's only little. Just like me," Penny pronounced proudly when she was taken into Spike's animal hospital. "Can I touch him, Spike. Please."

"I'll tell you what. Why don't I let you feed him? That way you can make friends."

Just then my mobile phone bleated, the ring tone notifying me it was a business call. "I have to take this," I said to Spike. Pushing my way out of the refuge for injured animals, I made my way down the hallway toward the back of the clinic, exiting through the double doors and out onto the sun deck. The view took my breath away. The front entrance to the vet clinic was unprepossessing, crowded among other bland shop fronts that blocked the spectacular view in the rear. There was a single lane asphalt roadway obviously used by garbage collection vehicles and people taking a shortcut to the rocky beach which lay below the grassy verge. Fishermen were casting their lines while pelicans lazed on the sandbanks as the tide came in.

I was so enamored of the view I'd neglected to speak until an irritated voice repeated "Hello. Hello," a number of times.

"Travis Black speaking. Sorry about the connection." I couldn't afford to get anyone offside. Anything that negatively affected my cash flow was to be avoided at all costs. "It's Kel Michaels here," the voice said.

I sighed. *There goes the weekend.*

"Is there a problem?"

Was there ever a problem. He chewed my ear off for a good fifteen minutes, his voice rising in volume until I thought he'd burst my eardrum. Kel Michaels was one unhappy man and he wanted to make sure I knew it. And also that I knew it was my fault. And that I'd ruined his weekend. And that I had to fix it pronto. Or else. His 'ands' went on and on before he finally got to the point. As it turned out, it wasn't my fault, he had changed his mind about what he wanted and I was expected to take the blame. That I would do in order that he could save face, but it would be added to his bill. I really wished I could add a surcharge for abuse and aggravation.

"I want the new version on my desk by this evening. Do you understand?"

"I understand," I replied in my most subservient tone even though it meant I would have to grab Penny and make tracks back the city immediately, something I knew she would not be prepared for without a fight. I wasn't looking forward to that. Had I been in a more secure financial position I would have told Mr. Kel Michaels to shove his demands, but I was neither that flush with ready cash nor with a reputation that could stand treating customers in such a cavalier manner.

He'd hung up before I could even get out my two words of capitulation. I sighed; this was not going to go well with Penny. I looked out over the lake wondering what life would be like waking to this view every day. Would I become so blasé I'd end up taking it for granted, barely noticing it until a stranger drew my attention to its delights. Did Spike appreciate what he had? He seemed such a calm, peaceful person I suspected he not only knew what he had but also cherished it. If only I had his equanimity.

I took a deep breath and turned my back on the view, determined to get the unpleasantness over as quickly as possible. I discovered Penny in the recovery section of the vet clinic where a number of cats and dogs, and one lonely guinea pig looked very sore and sorry, some sporting bandaged broken limbs. Penny was petting those that Spike obviously felt were safe enough, dispensing her childish love and concern. I watched from the doorway as Spike took her around to introduce her to each and every creature. It would have been cruel to interrupt before the introductions were completed. I waited impatiently, the seconds dribbling through the deadline hourglass much too quickly.

Eventually, they noticed me standing there, Penny running over to tug me toward some of her favorites to introduce me personally. It was taking forever and Spike could read the impatience in my face and body language. "Is something wrong?" he whispered.

"We have to go. Emergency."

"I hope no one is hurt," he replied, his face a map of concern.

"No. Just have to change a design for a client's website."

Spike almost exploded. "What? You call that an emergency?"

Penny looked up briefly before returning to the puppy that was whimpering hopefully that she would pet him again.

"It is to me. He's threatened to cancel the contract if it's not on his desk by this evening. The contract is big money; it's what is just about keeping us afloat financially. If I lose it, we're sunk."

He calmed down when he saw how seriously I needed this job. "You can use my desk top if that helps."

I shook my head. "I should have brought my laptop with me. It has everything I need on it. What a fuckwit to leave it at home."

"Today was your quality time with Penny. You didn't need any distractions."

"Now that quality time is going to be cut short because I didn't anticipate. Stupid. Stupid. Stupid."

"No use beating yourself up over it." Spike took a deep breath so I knew he was about to add something that he wasn't sure about. "How long will the job take?"

"About an hour. Give or take."

Spike looked at his watch. "It's still early. Why don't you leave Penny here with me, drive back, make the changes, and come back and stay the night? Bring your laptop with you just in case."

"I can't do that. I hardly know you."

"I can show you references if that's what you're worried about."

I was quick to reassure him. "No, it's not that. I couldn't possibly impose. I've only just met you."

Spike took a really deep breath. "Maybe it's love at first sight." His face turned crimson.

"Did you just come on to me?"

"Um, I might have. Yeah, I think I did. Crazy, huh?"

"I'm a married man." I realized how dumb that sounded after it came out of my mouth.

"Yeah, I get that a lot," Spike smiled.

"You have a fetish for married men?"

"Yes. Oh god, no. That's all I seen to get around here. It's not intentional. Guys holidaying with their families. Quick, no strings attached romp in the sand. That seems to be all I'm good for. Sorry, I didn't mean to offend."

"You didn't."

"No?"

"I'm flattered. What about Debbie in the fish shop?"

"Oh, I'm such an idiot. Of course, it's only natural you'd fancy her."

"Hold your horses. I thought the way she looked at you that, you know, you and her…"

"Hell, no. We're just good friends. She's got a crush on me but she knows the score. Hasn't stopped her from trying though. We're both unlucky in love."

"So, you're gay?"

Spike felt around his body as if searching for something. "Yep. I just checked, Looks as if I am."

I was shocked. "And you thought I was?"

"I thought there was a chance."

I was pissed off now. "Do I look gay to you?"

"Whoa, Mr. Straight-and-Narrow. There is no such thing as 'looking gay' unless you mean flamboyant and, even, then, a good proportion of those guys are straight. Maybe bi. It was just a vibe I got about you. Sorry if I got it wrong. I'm not looking for a broken nose from some uptight I'm-too-hetero-to-appreciate-a-gay-guy-cruising-me dude."

"I am not uptight."

"Then maybe you should take that poker out of your ass and relax a little."

"I haven't had anything up my ass in years. Not since I met Penny's mum." I sighed.

"Wait a second…"

I laughed.

"You asshole." He attempted to look angry but it came across more as a smirk. It was cute. He was cute. I'd only just noticed it.

"I switched that part of my brain off when I married. It was no big deal. I was in love. I thought it was for life. Turns out it wasn't."

"So what have you done for…um…fun since your wife left?" I wiggled the fingers on my right hand in reply. Spike bumped shoulders with me. "I sure would like to help you break that drought. So, how about my idea?"

I liked it. A lot. "I'll have to see if Penny agrees. She can be uncomfortable around strangers."

"Okay."

I called Penny over. "Honey, daddy has to go back home. Something important has come up."

She stamped her foot in annoyance. "I don't want to go back home. I want to stay here."

I recognized that behavior. If I attempted to budge her then it would degenerate into full-blown screaming and then, when she realized she wasn't going to win, it would become no speaking and, finally, sarcasm. I simply didn't have the energy.

Spike took over. "Penny, how would you like to stay here with me while your daddy goes home and does his work. It's important or he wouldn't go. It pays a lot of money so you can have pretty things and somewhere to live. Do you understand?"

She remained petulant. "Daddy works too hard. He's always working. He doesn't have enough time for me anymore."

I sensed a lot of pent-up frustration in my daughter. It was best not to go there at present. I saved it for discussion at a more opportune – and more private – moment.

Spike tried again. "Would you like to stay here with the animals until your daddy gets back? Then we can have dinner and you can sleep here tonight, then help me feed the pelicans tomorrow."

At the mention of pelicans, Penny's eyes lit up, her huff over. "Can we, daddy? Please, can we?"

I wasn't going to give in that easily. "Will you be a good girl while I'm gone and do everything Spike tells you?"

She looked very serious; she thought it made her look more grown-up. "Of course. I know how to behave myself."

Spike intervened. "It's settled then." Turning to me, he added, "The sooner you leave the sooner you'll be back." He shook his head when I hesitated. "She'll be fine. Stop worrying."

I kissed Penny, telling her again to be a 'good girl,' receiving an impatient sigh in return. Leaving her to the injured animals, Spike walked me outside to the car. I gave him my mobile number for emergencies and he handed me his vet's business card, adding "Don't think our little talk is over."

"You sure are persistent," I groused.

"Especially when I see something…or someone I want."

I drove off with a smile on my face. And, to my surprise, an erection in my trousers. Damn, I must like the guy. As I headed toward the expressway back to the city, I wondered what Spike would be like snuggled against me in bed. The fantasy obviously appealed to my lower regions because I had to adjust myself for fear of testicular strangulation. I'd need to change my briefs when I got home, I could feel a slight dampness in my crotch. Horny bugger, I chastised myself. There was no disguising what I thought would happen later that evening. I was gonna get my end in. My lonely nights of beating off while Penny was asleep in her room were about to be interrupted in a spectacular fashion, even if only for a weekend.

The journey, spent in a Technicolor romantic fantasy, was so swift I was surprised when I pulled up outside the ageing apartment block we now called home. I ignored the odor of piss and puke in the elevator up to the fifth floor, scarcely noticing the broken furniture that littered the hallway where occupants dumped it, hoping someone would cart it away for them. It never happened, the landlord was indifferent to the crumbling conditions in his building. Nothing, it seems, could dampen my good mood, and I made the necessary revisions, sending them off to the fussy client well within his deadline. Packing my laptop, stowing it on the back seat of the car, I was back on the road in less than two hours since I'd left Penny with Spike.

The client rang before I reached the expressway and I pulled over to the side of the road at the first opportunity. He was very happy with what I'd done, complimenting me on the speed in which I'd corrected the 'mistakes' and suggesting he would be sending more work in my direction. I pumped my fist in triumph, glad that he couldn't see me.

Once back on the road, my more cautious nature began to push to the fore. Did I really want to become involved with a man?

Involved? It's a one-weekend stand.

How will I explain it to Penny?

What's to explain? You'll be doing it in the privacy of Spike's bedroom.

What about Debbie at the fish and chips shop? She's hot.

Yeah, she is. But Spike is so easy. He's ready for it like I am. With Debbie I'd have to wine and dine and seduce her. Spike is begging for it now.

Debbie would make a great mother for Penny.

Mmm, there is that.

I didn't know my subconscious was on the lookout for a new mum for my daughter. I didn't recall ever consciously thinking about it. Maybe I should. It would help with my business. There were opportunities I'd had to turn down in the past because they were not compatible with bringing up a young girl. There was no denying Penny's welfare had cruelled many a chance of advancement. Not that I minded. Penny was the light of my life. Besides, we were making ends meet at the moment. Just. It was that 'just' that had me kowtowing to the Kel Michaels' demands no matter how unreasonable they were. I wouldn't have Spike to help me out next time. Maybe a wife would be the answer. But where to start?

Debbie, my subconscious reiterated.

By the time I returned to the coastal town, I was having second thoughts about Spike although my dick remained firmly convinced it was in for a treat that night. It would brook no argument. Spike must have heard me drive up because he opened the door as I got out of the car, taking my laptop with me. "More work?" he queried.

"Nah, this is so I don't have to make any more emergency dashes to the city. How's Penny?"

"She's been a little angel."

"If that's the case, aliens have slipped in while you weren't looking and reprogrammed her. Angelic is not a description I ever would have used. I hope she hasn't been a nuisance."

"Not at all. I like having her here."

"More than most people do," I said as I went inside to dump my computer and the small bag of change of clothes in the dining area. "Penny is one of the reasons I gave up dating after my wife left. She didn't like any of the women I brought home to meet her. Any more than they liked her. No one wants a ready-made family. Particularly a sulking girl with a sarcastic tongue. I know, in the beginning, it was because she missed her mum…"

"She doesn't visit?"

I shook my head. "No maternal instincts. As soon as the divorce was finalized, she sold the house and headed who knows where? Cut all contact. I know Penny misses having a mother."

"What about two fathers? Scientific studies have shown—"

"I'd never put Penny through that."

Spike looked shocked and disappointed at the vehemence of my response. "Sorry, that came out a bit more adamant than I meant. Besides, even less chance a dude will want to be saddled with a daughter."

"I don't know…"

This conversation was headed into dangerous territory and I needed to stop it now. "Where is she?"

Spike seemed as relieved as I was at the change of subject. "She's watching *The Little Mermaid* on DVD.

"That's her favorite."

Spike laughed. "I guessed as much. She's been singing along with every song."

"You sure we're not putting you out?"

"I should tell you, my Saturday nights consist of watching a movie, ordering a pizza, and drinking myself stupid until I don't feel the pain of my useless existence."

"Anything but useless." I brushed my fingers across his cheek. "You're much more use to the world than I am. You save lives. Make people happy."

He stepped into my personal space, placing his hands around my lower back. "What makes you happy, Travis?"

I really didn't have an answer to that so I masked it by leaning forward to kiss him. It was exploratory. Sweet and gentle, lips and tongues, before we opened up to allow the other in for a deeper commitment, more passion. We dueled for supremacy but it was a competition that neither of us cared about, taking turns at domination. When we broke for breath I said, "Wow. You kiss like you mean it."

"I do," he responded. "It's been a long time since I've met someone who kisses as well as you do."

I needed to get something straight. "Spike, this is only for a weekend. It can't be anything else."

"I understand," he said. "But the city is not that far…"

He left it hanging so I ignored the implications. He pecked me on the cheek before disengaging my arms. "I hope you like spaghetti. Penny said it's one of her favorites."

"You don't have to go to any trouble. We can order in. I'm happy to pay for it. After all, you've done babysitter duties."

"I enjoy cooking but I can't get much enthusiasm when it's just for me. This is the perfect opportunity. Besides, it's pretty basic. You can't go wrong with pasta."

"Can't you?" I laughed. "I've been known to burn water."

"Daddy," Penny screamed, running into the dining area. "Spike's making 'ghetti for dinner."

As if it were a signal, the timer went off in the kitchen. "Looks as if it's ready. Why don't you sit Penny up at the table, and I'll serve."

"Need some help in the kitchen?" I asked as I settled Penny onto the chair that had been padded with a number of cushions to elevate her enough to reach the forks and spoons.

"Wouldn't mind."

I trailed Spike and he got me to strain the pasta which I then poured into a large bowl. He added the simmering pasta sauce and gently mixed the ingredients before taking a tray of garlic bread out of the oven. "Look, Travis. I like you but don't feel pressured into anything tonight. Penny can have the spare room but if you don't want to...you know, then I can sleep on the lounge tonight. As I said—"

I stuffed a warm piece of garlic bread in his mouth to shut him up. "Does it mean I'll get more of those sweet kisses if I share your bed?"

"Hell, yeah. I'd be content just to do that if that's all you felt like."

"I want to see if you taste as sweet all over." I took the opportunity to swat his ass as I took the bread to the table. A simple rocket and roast pumpkin salad with goat's cheese was already in place, Penny stabbing at the creamy white crumbs with her fork.

"Manners, Penny," I chastised.

"What is it, daddy?"

"That's grown-ups salad," Spike said. "Here, I brought one specially for you." He placed a small bowl of shredded iceberg lettuce and cherry tomatoes next to her plate.

"I'm grown up," she said, eyeing the adult salad with suspicion.

"How about I give you a little to try?" Spike said, placing the bowl of steaming spaghetti on the table. "Your dad can serve you while I get you a little bit of grown-up salad."

I used the tongs to dish out three portions of pasta while Spike scooped up a couple of rocket leaves and a small portion of goat's cheese and placed it in Penny's own bowl. I knew that would make her feel very grown up. I speared a small portion of pumpkin, adding it to the mix. I also gave her two pieces of garlic bread. It was never a good idea to deny Penny anything I was eating.

"I must say, this sauce is one of the best I've ever tasted. What's your secret?" I said, genuinely impressed.

"As long as you promise not to tell."

I crossed my heart.

Spike whispered as if imparting the most secret of information. "Aisle three at the local supermarket, about half-way along the shelves on the right. A whole collection of genuine bottled pasta sauces."

He smiled at my discomfort. He probably thought I was sucking up. "It must be the way you pour it then because the ones I buy never taste this good."

"It must be the company that makes it special."

Before I could say anything, he nodded toward Penny who was venturing to try the rocket salad. She screwed her face up, "Yuck."

"I'll remind you of this moment when you grow up and insist you've always loved rocket and goat's cheese," I said.

"Never going to happen," Penny retorted, spooning spaghetti into her mouth but smearing errant tomato sauce all over her chin in the process.

The meal was pleasant – much too pleasant for my liking as I could really get used to it – and I was pleased that Spike went out of his way to include Penny in the conversation, seemingly interested in her every utterance, so much so I could easily have become jealous. But he turned his attention to me whenever I felt neglected. Smooth. After the meal, he won Penny over with a bowl of mango gelato while he and I settled for the more astringent lemon/lime variety.

Penny returned to the living room to finish watching her movie while I washed up and Spike dried because he knew where each item needed to be put away. Conversation was easy and he told me about his love of animals which steered him into his career while I revealed that I had been – probably still was – a computer nerd. My career chose me because I was hopeless at anything else. It was either computers or unemployment. By the time we went to join Penny she was asleep on the lounge, her arms wrapped tightly around one of the cushions.

"I'll put her to bed." Picking her up in my arms, I carried her down the hallway to the bedroom Spike had made up especially for her. "You have sheets with pelicans on them?" I said to Spike once I'd tucked Penny into bed, and kissed her good night. I left the bedroom door ajar just in case she woke up during the night and was frightened by the unfamiliar surroundings.

"Doesn't everyone?" he smirked.

"What are you, a pelican shape shifter?"

"I wish," he replied. "You want a beer?"

"Thanks." I settled on the lounge while he went to the kitchen. "What are we watching?"

We only lasted the first twenty minutes of some movie I don't even remember, sitting side by side as we swigged our beers, getting hornier by the minute.

"Fuck this," Spike said finally. "Are you having as hard a time concentrating as I am?"

"Uh huh."

He grabbed my hand to pull me toward his bedroom. I tugged free to check that Penny was still sound asleep, while he took the opportunity to lock up and switch off the lights. Eagerness was overtaken by shyness once we were in his room, both reluctant to strip in front of the other. My body is just average. I have a muffin top around the waist. I suppose I could get a gym membership but I'd never have an opportunity to use it although it would probably help if I cut down on the snack foods while I'm at the computer. I've had no one to impress of late so I've let myself go a little. God, I hoped it wasn't a turn-off. What if Spike only liked those bulging arms and chests you see on hot guys? I was bound to be a major disappointment. Where did I get the idea this was going to work?

Spike must have had less trepidation because he was stripped to his jockeys, his muscular body without an ounce of fat that I could see, but with an encouraging bulge outlined in his underwear. What the fuck, what's the most he could do? Puke his lungs out at the sight of my less than perfect body? Well, he didn't. He whistled his appreciation, "You're fucking gorgeous."

"The admiration is mutual," I said.

We both slipped under the sheets in our undies, discarding them once we were covered. Stupid really because he immediately put his hand around my hard prick and I did the same. "Mm, nice," I murmured. Spike didn't say much at all because he'd already relinquished my dick and slid under the sheet to engulf my hard-on in his warm mouth.

I was so startled by the suddenness of his move I squealed as I felt his tongue against the shaft. I lay back and groaned. It had been a long time for me although I didn't remember it ever being this good before. Spike was obviously an expert. He could give lessons. I wondered whether I'd be up to his standards as it had been more than five years since I'd sucked cock. Maybe he wouldn't want that, maybe he'd want to stick…I panicked. What if I couldn't do it anymore?

"Relax," Spike said, slapping my thigh to get my attention. "We don't have to do anything you don't want to."

"What are you? A mind reader?"

"I know performance anxiety when I see it." Chuckling, he went back to work, rolling his lips down the shaft until he could go no further, his nose wedged in my pubic hair, my cock penetrating his throat. I ran my fingers through his hair wanting nothing more than to hold his head in place while I fucked his mouth. As if he could read my mind, he relinquished his throat hold on my dick to say, "You can if you want to. I like it rough sometimes. I'm probably not like the women you date. You don't have to take it easy. I won't break."

When he went back to suck my cock again, I did hold his head still while I attacked his mouth and his throat. Occasionally, I would take him by surprise and change the angle, making him gag slightly. I relaxed and let him take over once again, set his own pace, although it had been wonderful to let rip for just a moment. All too soon I was on the edge and I mumbled, "Um…Spike. Slow down, otherwise…"

That merely spurred him on and in no time at all I was squirting my load down his throat. I felt his throat muscles squeezing my dick as he swallowed every drop. When I'd shot my load, he cleaned me up by licking the last droplets from the head of my prick. "A-ma-zing," I panted as I lay back against the pillows. "Give me a few minutes and I'll return the favor."

"Um…what I'd really like to do…"

I looked up and into his eager eyes. "It's been a long time."

"Is that a 'no'?"

"Just a request to take it slow."

"Okay." He fumbled in the bedside table and produced a strip of condoms and a small bottle of lube. "I hope these haven't expired," he said examining the foil wrappers. "Phew. Two months before they lapse." He held them out for me to see but I waved him away. "I trust you."

I lay on my back, my legs pulled back toward my chest, giving him free rein to my ass. He unscrewed the bottle to pour a goodly amount of lubricating gel into his hand before slicking up his middle finger which he ran around my anal ring to grease its entry before pushing inside. I barely felt it so he added a second. My anus tightened at the intrusion but a drop more lube and a little more perseverance and he pushed inside. It felt good. I'd forgotten how much I enjoyed it. The third finger was more painful but I could bear it and once he'd anally gate crashed, prodding gently for a few moments, I got used to accommodating the intrusion.

With his free hand, Spike picked up the strip of condoms and tore one open with his teeth, sheathing the rubber over his erection before greasing it up for easier entry. He removed his fingers before lining up his cock, waiting until I nodded I was ready. He pushed, and my sphincter attempted to prevent his entry. But not for long. His persistence paid off and soon the head was embedded inside me. He paused until I nodded again and then slid slowly all the way inside.

"Fuck, that feels so good," I said as he filled me totally. Relaxing my muscles, I allowed him easier access each time he withdrew to push back inside, opening me up for rougher treatment later on. "This is just until you get used to it," he said.

"Don't just talk about it. Do it. Do me hard. I want to feel it."

"Oh, you will."

He began slowly, picking up speed and like a steam locomotive until he was pounding me like he was trying to split me in two. "That's it," I encouraged. "Show me how much you like my ass."

"I like your ass just fine," he panted. "Once I finish with you then you'll never be satisfied with anyone else."

"Smug bastard." I moaned because he was hitting all the correct internal spots to get my dick hard again, almost making me beg for it. I guess he knew without me saying it because he began to fuck harder and rougher until I would have sworn we'd make a hole in the mattress and fall through to the floor below. I loved the way he played my ass and my entire body, nibbling on my nipples as he slowed the pace because he was close to coming. I felt his heart thumping in his chest, or maybe that was my own.

He remained still, wedged tight inside me until the edge retreated and he could once again bang my ass. I don't think either of us was looking for love and schmaltz at that precise moment, we were overwhelmed by the sheer exuberance of animal fucking. I clamped my sphincter around his cock forcing little whimpering sounds from him as he pounded me, feeling my own orgasm churning in my balls.

"I don't think…" I said but I never got to finish the sentence because spunk shot out of my prick onto my belly and chest, the pulsating in my ass bringing Spike off a few moments later. We were both puffing from the exertion.

"Fucking hell, Travis."

I had only enough energy to agree. "Yeah."

He leaned over the side of the bed to dispose of the condom and to retrieve his jockeys, wiping the sticky mess from my chest and from his own. Neither of us had the will to make it to the bathroom for a warm wash cloth. I snuggled against his back and was soon fast asleep. It was still dark outside when I was awoken by the feel of something warm and wet against my cock. I was disorientated for a moment until I remembered I was in Spike's bed.

I wasn't spooning him any longer, in fact he wasn't in the bed at all as I felt around for him. Obviously, he'd got up to wipe the dried sperm off our bodies and was currently wiping my cock. Uh uh. That felt like a tongue.

"What the…"

"Morning, sleepy."

"I don't think I have any cum left. The tank's empty." My cock didn't care particularly whether there was any spunk to be siphoned off because it was hard as steel. That's all Spike was waiting for. He was fast as lightning and had my dick sheathed in a rubber and greased up before I could say anything. He'd obviously already prepped his own ass because he squatted above my very wide awake organ and lowered himself deftly down to my balls, sighing in contentment.

"Your ass is so hot," I said, pushing up into him. Not my favorite position but I wasn't about to complain. Spike rode me, dragging his sphincter up and down my shaft, squeezing to get every last drop of sperm out of me although I wasn't sure whether it was a futile effort or not. Seems not because I felt a twitch in my balls as if the spermatozoon manufacturing plant had been working overtime. If I was going to bust my balls I was going to get my fun as well. I shoved Spike backwards, keeping my cock embedded in his ass until his legs were around my waist and I was in the right position to fuck him senseless. I pounded like his ass was raw beef until with a loud grunt I unloaded into the condom inside him, while he jerked his dick to climax, splattering all over his chest and chin.

We flopped together exhausted and I didn't wake up until I felt someone tugging on my arm. I opened my bleary eyes.

"Daddy. Wake up. I'm hungry."

Shit, I meant to be out of bed before Penny got up. I took a quick peek to ensure the Spike and I were covered – phew! – before I told Penny to go and wait in the living room and that I'd be out shortly to make her something nice. Our conversation woke Spike who pulled the sheet more tightly around his neck.

"Morning, Spike," Penny said cheerily as she left the bedroom as if there was nothing wrong with her daddy sharing a bed with another man. I guess she equated it with a sleep over like she had sometimes with her girlfriends.

"I meant to set the alarm," I moaned.

"No harm done," Spike said. "It didn't seem to faze her."

"At least we were covered up."

"That's not what I meant."

"What did you mean then?"

"What do you think I mean?" There was a definite sarcastic strain to Spike's voice.

"You meant that she didn't see anything wrong with her daddy being in bed with a man rather than a woman. Right?" I sneered.

"As a matter of fact, yes." Spike climbed out of bed and was into the bathroom before I could scoff at his answer. I heard the shower. I suppose I could have joined him to try to make things right between us, but I didn't. It would serve no purpose. I would never see Spike again after today so it hardly mattered what he thought of me. Still…

While I was dithering, I heard the shower turn off and a few minutes later Spike emerged, his hair disheveled and damp, a towel wrapped around his waist. "The bathroom's free," he said coldly. "You'll find a new toothbrush in the cabinet behind the mirror. Help yourself to anything you need."

"This is not how I wanted it to end," I muttered as I took refuge from Spike's anger and turned the spray on my aching body. I remained in the shower longer than necessary hoping he'd be gone from the bedroom by the time I'd cleaned my teeth and dried myself. He was. After I dressed I found him in the kitchen making pancakes.

"Daddy," Penny cried enthusiastically, "Spike is going to let me be his assistant at the pelican feeding this afternoon."

I glared at him but he ignored me. "Honey, I don't think we can stay that late today. You have school tomorrow. Daddy has a lot of work to get finished."

"You can sit here and work at the table," Spike said. "I have Wi-Fi."

"Daddy, you said we could feed the pelicans today. You promised."

I remembered making some half-hearted promise that we might come back but I had no intention of honoring that.

"Looks like daddy's a bit of a liar," Spike said from the kitchen.

"That's not helping," I snapped. "I have important work to do." It sounded feeble even to my ears.

"I thought that's why you brought your laptop," Spike said.

"Can I see you inside for a moment," I hissed at Spike.

"I'm making pancakes for breakfast," he replied.

I took the spatula from his hand. "That can wait."

I think he realized from my tone that we were way past the negotiating phase.

He threw the other kitchen implements into the sink and strode off toward the bedroom.

"Now look what you've done, daddy. You've made Spike angry. And you've made me angry, too." She folded her arms to show she meant business.

I had enough drama in my life without these two adding to it. I followed Spike into the bedroom, closing the door behind me.

"I'm sorry," we both said at once.

"I didn't mean to insult you," I added.

"I shouldn't have over-reacted," he said.

Dragging him to me, I kissed him. I hadn't been mistaken, his kisses were sweeter than any I'd ever had before. His body relaxed and the anger all drained out of him. One kiss and I wondered why I was arguing with this incredible man. For a second I wished he was a woman, eternally grateful that he couldn't read my mind because that would have been so insulting there was no apologizing for a gaffe like that.

"Friends?" I asked.

"Friends."

I'm not sure where the conversation would have led because Penny screamed from the kitchen.

"Daddy, something's burning."

"Oh, shit," Spike said. "The pancakes."

It was mid-morning before we'd managed to get the smell out of the house and we'd scrubbed the pan clean to make another batch, Penny having long ago filled up on some sugary breakfast cereal Spike found unopened in his pantry. She was happy to sit and watch television on the promise of pancakes later.

Spike and I bumped hips and shoulders like young teenagers as we made what was now brunch. He had the more skilled task of pancake manufacture while I was assigned the simpler job of cutting up strawberries and keeping an eye on the pancakes already made that were kept warm in the oven.

I must admit, Spike manufactured an amazing breakfast for three from the skimpiest of ingredients even if his strawberry pancakes had to be augmented with strawberry jam. Penny's were topped off with chocolate ice cream while Spike and I enjoyed ours with vanilla.

While I washed up, Spike had to attend to his animals, taking Penny with him. Once I'd dried the plates and implements, stacking them in their correct drawers and shelves, I sat at the table and opened the computer. I was so engrossed in catching up on email correspondence and getting together a résumé and prospective ideas for a forthcoming conference that it wasn't until Penny returned that I realized it would soon be time for them to leave for the public pelican feeding.

"I fed Pontus today, daddy. I think he likes me."

"He likes you a lot," Spike said.

"Are you still mad at Spike, Daddy?" Penny demanded.

"No, honey. We just had a little disagreement. Everything's fine now."

"Then let me see you kiss and make up."

Spike and I both looked at each other in shock.

"We can't do that," I spluttered.

"Why not?" she demanded. "My friends and I do that all the time after we have a fight."

"But we're two men," I explained. As soon as the words were out of my mouth I knew I'd said the wrong thing.

"Come on, Penny. We'll go and feed Pontus and leave your dad to his work."

She stood her ground. "No. Not until you kiss and make up."

There was absolutely no use in arguing. "Come here," I said.

I saw the look that said Spike wasn't about to budge and that I'd have to go over to him. I wasn't prepared to argue so petty a point so I went over and kissed him on the cheek.

"No, daddy. Like you really mean it."

I put my arms around him before rubbing my nose against his cheek and then planted a kiss. I felt a twitch in my trousers and, if I wasn't mistaken, a corresponding twitch in his. I hadn't been this horny since I was a teenager. What was it about this guy that pushed all my buttons?

"That's better. Now, say 'sorry.' Go on."

"I'm sorry, Spike."

"Now your turn," she said.

""Sorry," Spike said.

"All better now."

Spike and I were still standing with our arms around each other. I liked the feeling. Neither of us could move because our erections would have been quite obvious. We would have to stand, locked like this, until our dicks went down and the way I felt, that could be months, if not years.

Spike saved the day. "Penny, could you do me a big favor? Could you go out and make sure that I locked Pontus's cage. I wouldn't want him to get out and injure himself."

Her enthusiasm for the task carried her out of the room and Spike and I broke to each adjust his cock to a more comfortable position. I wanted to give him a real kiss but I knew I'd be sunk if I did that and my dick would never go down.

"Will I ever see you again after you leave today?" he asked.

I was non-committal. "Do you think that's a good idea?"

He took it as the rejection I intended without actually saying it in so many words.

"Ah, well. I had a really good time last night. You know where I live. You have my phone number."

I worked steadily, grateful that Spike kept Penny occupied with his menagerie because it enabled me to concentrate on the task at hand instead of Penny's usual constant interruptions. I didn't begrudge her but it meant it usually took twice as long to complete important projects. This way, I was ready to join them when they went to perform the public feeding, Penny wallowing in self-importance as Spike's assistant. I must admit to feeling pride while I watched her feeding the pelicans and, I guessed, there were many a girl and boy who would have given anything to be in her place that day.

It was with the utmost reluctance that I managed to drag her away in the late afternoon for the journey back home. "Why can't we stay here?" she complained.

"Because this is Spike's home."

"There's plenty of room," he said cheerfully.

"Not helping," I spat at him.

"There's plenty of room, daddy. I have my own bedroom and you and Spike can share the other one. Like last night."

That brought back the image of Spike impaled on my cock. I suddenly had to put my laptop in front of my crotch so I wouldn't shock the locals.

"Maybe you can get your daddy to bring you back for a visit some time. You can see how Pontus is getting on. I think he likes you."

"Not fair," I said.

"Can we, daddy?"

"We'll see."

There was no opportunity for any passionate farewells although I felt like I was being gutted as we drove away. I could see Spike waving until the car turned a corner and he disappeared from sight. Suddenly, the atmosphere in the car changed, a patina of melancholy settled over both of us.

"Can we visit Spike again, daddy?" Penny asked although with such a sense of disappointment in her voice as if she already knew the answer. Best to get it out the way at once. "I don't think so, honey. Daddy will be very busy for the next few months."

She didn't say anything and remained quiet for the rest of the trip home. I didn't feel so good myself. The melancholy mood seemed to pervade our lives over the next week or so even though I spent more time with Penny than usual. She didn't seem to appreciate it except as extra time in which to bombard me with questions and opinions about Spike. It got to the stage where I never wanted to hear his name again. That was only because of what his name did to my groin. My dreams were an entirely different matter and I woke up each morning with a Spike-induced hard-on hoping it was his lips making me feel so good instead of just my hand.

The one good thing to come out of that weekend was my determination to begin dating again, hoping to find a suitable mother for Penny. No use pretending it was easy, but made doubly difficult by Penny's total antipathy to any female who came within spitting distance, and her always moaning, "Why can't we go and see Spike and Pontus?"

I must admit I thought about Spike more than I did any of the women I dated. I slept with a few of them – to our mutual satisfaction – but it was always Spike

I imagined under me as I penetrated them. Most guessed that my mind was elsewhere, some probably even guessing where when I reached to jerk off their non-existent cock. I gave in after one disastrous night when I couldn't even manage to get hard and satisfied my date with my tongue. On that occasion, thinking about Spike didn't do the trick. His image was beginning to fade in my mind.

"Hello?" the familiar voice said.

"Hi." It was a feeble response

"Travis?"

"Yeah. How are you doing?"

"Still single," he hinted. "You?"

"The same."

"What can I do for you?"

"Penny's been nagging me—"

He chuckled. "She's good at that."

"She wants to see Pontus again. Do you still have him?"

"He got an infection. Almost died. But he's getting better."

"So, are you free on the weekend?"

"Saturday or Sunday?"

"Either." Long pause. "Or…um…maybe both."

"Both would be good. You got anywhere to stay?"

"Not yet."

"Then you must stay here."

"Um…"

"It's okay," he said. "I'll sleep on the couch."

I couldn't keep the disappointment from my voice. "Oh."

"What?"

"Maybe we could…"

"Maybe we could what?"

"You know?"

"Know what?"

He was going to force me to say it.

"Maybe we could sort of do what we did before."

"You mean, fuck?"

"Yeah."

I heard the smile in his voice. "Maybe we could."

That weekend we made like rabbits although there would be no reproduction from our constant coupling. The passion was still there. The incredible sex hadn't diminished. Nor did it in the following weeks and months during which Penny and I made the trek north to spend weekends with Spike. I even moved in some of my shaving gear and my own toothbrush and left a change of underwear. Debbie at the fish and chip shop sighed theatrically every time we walked in to buy lunch. She went too far the day she said, "Look at you two. If you were any more in love, it would be sickening."

I guess she forgot Penny was there because I saw my daughter look at us strangely. But Debbie's statement was a wake-up call. Spike knew there was something wrong the moment we stepped outside. "It doesn't mean anything," he said. But I was having an anxiety attack. Did people think Spike and I were a couple? Is that how Spike saw us?

Back at his house I sent Penny outside to play with Pontus who was now a free agent although he hung around the house because his wing had not healed properly, Spike concerned he would never be able to fend for himself. Penny had adopted him and frequently asked why we couldn't take Pontus back to the city with us. Spike and I sat on the back porch watching her play a sort of pelican tag.

"It's okay," Spike said. "I know what you're going to say."

"How? The look on my face when Debbie dropped her clanger?"

"It wasn't a clanger, you know. She's quite right what she said. At least in regard to my feelings."

I really didn't want to ask. "What do you mean?"

"You're not a stupid man, Travis. You must know how I feel about you."

"I guess I do."

"And?"

"I have feelings for you."

"That's something, I suppose. But not enough. Each time you and Penny leave it rips my heart out. I want you both in my life, here with me…"

"I can't. I have a business…"

"Which you could just as successfully run from here. You said so yourself once when we were sitting in this exact same spot."

"I can't. Penny."

"You're just using her as an excuse. But until you can see that, Travis. I don't think you should visit anymore."

"Wait. What?"

"Isn't that what you were going to say to me? That it's over?"

"Yes, but I thought you'd beg me to stay."

"If I have to beg, it's worthless."

He stood up. "I'm going to do the pelican feeding now. When I come back, I'd prefer it if you weren't here."

"What do I tell Penny?"

"How about the truth."

He was gone.

Penny cried the entire trip, blaming me for never seeing Spike or Pontus again. "I'll run away," she said defiantly. And I was afraid she might.

My resolve wavered a few times. I came close to calling Spike but it would have been of little value as I hadn't changed my mind about anything. I'd taken to serious dating this time, farming Penny out to babysitters I could ill afford in order to test the waters with these women. I genuinely liked a few of them. 'Liked' being the operative word. There was no spark. In fact, the more I dated, the more it brought home to me how much I more than liked Spike. I just wasn't prepared to go there.

Circumstances change and about three months after our break-up, I was forced to ring him.

"Hi," I said sheepishly.

"Hi." His response was cool.

"I wouldn't ask but I need the biggest favor ever."

"I guess it was too much to ask that you might be ringing about…something else."

"I'm sorry."

"You're always sorry."

"Look, I'm desperate."

"Thanks," he said sarcastically. "But in case you hadn't noticed, I'm not a charity."

"No, you're a beautiful human being and I just wish I could let all the baggage go and do what my feelings tell me. But I can't."

"You can fuck me but you can't love me, is that it?"

"I do love you, Spike."

"You just can't do it publicly, is that it?"

"It's complicated."

"Isn't it always?"

"Look, this call was a bad idea." I was about to apologize again but I don't think I could have stood his sarcasm at that moment.

"What was it you wanted?"

"It's too much to ask."

"I'll be the judge of that."

Taking a deep breath, I launched into my last hope. "I have a five-day meet and greet for what could be the client that gets Penny and me out of the muck and into a fairly decent life. It's big money. Really big money. But the company has invited all the competing businesses to make their sales pitch at this resort, all expenses paid. I have to go to be in the running. None of Penny's sitters can take her for such a long period and, quite frankly, I couldn't afford them if they could…"

"You want me to look after Penny? Of course, I will. When is it?"

"You will? I'll be so grateful. It's really short notice."

I explained the details, telling him I would bring Penny up the following Sunday but ensuring he knew that I would not be staying. "I do miss you, Spike."

"But not enough."

"No."

"Travis, I'm happy to do this for Penny's sake but I will make one request."

"Anything."

"After you come back from your five-day seminar or whatever it's called, and you pick up Penny, don't ever contact me again."

Even though it ripped my heart out, I said, "Understood."

The reception when I took an enthusiastic Penny to Spike's place was cool but not antagonistic. I left as quickly and unobtrusively as I could to drive back to the city. I'd go straight to the airport to catch a plane to the resort where my future would be decided. If I could win this against some of the toughest bastards in the business then I would be able to drag us up out of the financial mire in which we were wallowing. If not, then I would have to get some sort of job to pay the bills, and I didn't like my chances in this market.

I had my future in my laptop as I boarded the jet and I was so tense I had too many red wines so that the cabin crew practically poured me off the aircraft at our destination. Fortunately, the company shouted us business class seats so the crew turned a blind eye to the maudlin soak in their midst.

On arrival at the resort I was met by Sonia, the woman handling the PR side of the five days. "Mr. Black, you certainly look as if you enjoyed your flight."

"Very much, thank you."

"You came alone?"

"I'm pretty much a one-man band."

Her eyebrow rose at that. I wondered if I'd said the wrong thing.

"I'll show you to your room." She took the key from the reception and led the way to the elevator, the bell boy bringing up the rear with my scant luggage. I was on the fifth floor, overlooking the pool, the room about three times the size of my apartment back home. While I was gazing out the window, feeling lost and alone, Sonia must have tipped the bellboy because the next thing I felt was her arms circling my chest. I didn't shrug her off because at that moment I needed companionship.

"You're the last arrival of the night so why don't you and I get to know each other a little better?"

Sonia had a voracious appetite for sex. She was as expert as Spike. I had to stop with the comparisons because, in this case, they were not as odious. She was the equal of Spike in every way with the added attraction of being female. I could quite easily become besotted. In fact, over the five days on constant interrogation by the company's elite and the stress of pitching my ideas, she was the one bright spot that relieved the tension. By the final night, I was ready to propose marriage. She was divorced and had a son about the same age as Penny. This was a match made in heaven.

I took extra care with my shower and shave in expectation of her nightly visit. First, though, we had to endure a company dinner at which the winning tender would be announced. I'd long since given up any hope of being successful. I'd seen a few of the other presentations and mine was amateur in comparison. It was agony enduring the meal, unable to taste the expense and opulence of the courses or the rare vintage wines that accompanied them, as I had my mind set on the proposal I intended for Sonia. Or the proposal I would have made had circumstances not prevented it.

My pitch was not successful, but having expected bad news it had only a minor effect on me. Perhaps I should not have drunk as much as I did because by the time I crawled back to my hotel room later that evening, I was puking my guts up. "There, get it all out," a kind voice said. "I don't know what's troubling you but you sure have yourself tied up in knots about it." Sonia handed me a face towel. "Want to talk about it?"

"Can you give me ten minutes?"

"Make it fifteen. And have a shower," she said.

I did, and felt much better for it. By the time I emerged, she had a strong black coffee and aspirin waiting for me. Normally, she sat next to me, her octopus hands ravaging my body until she'd removed all my clothes. Tonight she sat in the armchair opposite.

"Anything I can do to help?"

I don't know what made me say it. "I know you'll laugh at me, but I was going to propose to you tonight."

"You'll probably laugh at me, but I would have accepted."

"Really?"

"Even though it would only end in misery for both of us."

"I realized that tonight."

"I find that at these sorts of events, men usually fuck around for the first day or two and then they start to miss home."

"Something like that. I have a daughter. Same age as your son."

"No, that's not it. There's someone else."

"Yes."

"She must be very special."

"He is."

"Ah."

"What does that mean?"

"You were married. Got a kid. You're either a late bloomer. Or you're bi."

"Bi. Always have been."

"Never thought you'd feel that way about a man. Can't explain it to your little girl so you're looking for a nice woman instead."

"You make it sound so callous."

"That's because it is."

I pleaded my case. "I genuinely like you."

"I like plum pudding but I wouldn't want to marry one."

"It's enough. I can build on that."

"Why? You already love someone. Does he love you back?"

"More than I deserve."

"Then what the fuck are you doing here?"

"I'm a coward."

She laughed. "But honest with it. Who said love was going to be easy? You gotta crawl and take baby steps until you learn how to walk on your own, like an adult."

I broke down. I was such a failure. I couldn't even get a proposal right. I was a pitiable drunk. I cried until the tears were all gone. She tucked me in bed, kissing me on the forehead. "That was a close call. No one deserves to be treated like that, Travis. Do the right thing."

"Thanks, Sonia. I'll never forget you."

"Name your first kid after me."

"What if it's a boy?"

"So what's wrong with Sonia?"

"Absolutely nothing."

I went to sleep a new man.

In the morning I rang the airport and changed my ticket for an earlier flight. Spike wasn't expecting me until that evening but I was back in the city a little after breakfast. Back at our apartment I packed a suitcase with my clothes and another with Penny's. I'd come back for the rest another day as long as everything panned out. I loaded the car and took off for the coast.

At Spike's place, I put the suitcases in the hallway because there was nothing to say he would welcome me but I had to take the chance. I heard sounds from the back lawn and I went out on the deck to watch Spike and Penny encouraging Pontus to fly. His crippled wing must have hurt because he hobbled about the lawn while they shouted encouragement. All he needed was the will to fly. He flapped his wings and attempted a take-off. It was bumpy but he managed to become airborne. He fluttered to earth, but after a few minutes rest, he tried again. He kept trying until, as the three of us watched, he finally made it into the air, buffeted by the breeze he made adjustments for his damaged wing. He flew lopsided for a while but then righted himself, flying out over the sand banks until he found a space amongst the pelicans lazing on the lake. He was home.

"Daddy," Penny screamed when she saw me standing watching. "Pontus flew away. Did you see? Did you see? I want to be a vet when I grow up. Can I, daddy? Please."

"You can be whatever you want. Okay?" I said lifting her up.

"Thanks, daddy." She kissed me on the cheek.

"Have you been a good girl for Spike while I was away?"

"Of course."

I had caught Spike's eyes as soon as he turned at the sound of my voice. I didn't turn away. "Honey, how would you feel if we moved from where we live now?"

"Could we move closer to Spike, daddy? I'd like that."

I saw hope flicker in his eyes.

"What would you think if you had two daddies?"

"You mean instead of a mummy and a daddy?"

"Exactly."

Spike was trying to smother a smile.

"Cool." She said. "Marcie at kindy has two mums and she says it's great. Kevin has two dads but he pretends one of them is his uncle but he doesn't fool anybody. Can Spike be my other daddy? Please say 'yes.' Please."

"That would be up to Spike."

"Of course he will, daddy. He likes you. Lots. Will you be my other daddy, Spike?"

"I'd be honored. But it's up to your main daddy. Is it what he wants?"

I walked over to the man I intended to spend the rest of my life with. The man I should have acknowledged as the love of my life months earlier. It wasn't too late. "I love you, Spike."

He put his arms around us, hugging us tightly, kissing my cheek.

"You're crushing me, daddy," Penny complained.

"Which one?" I laughed as I put her back down.

"Both of you, silly."

I took Spike's hand and we followed her back into our new home.

Lydian Press

ABOUT THE AUTHOR

Barry Lowe writes about love and sex so he won't forget how to do it. When he's not out doing field research, he's writing about love's wonderful variations for a series of smut eBooks, novels and anthologies for Lydian Press

Go to www.barrylowe.info

OTHER WORKS BY BARRY LOWE

Available in eBook and Print

PLAYS

THE DEATH OF PETER PAN: Gay Historical Romance

NOVELS & ANTHOLOGIES

BUSTING BILLY'S BUTT: A Gay Erotic Romance

Steve and Billy's monogamous relationship has gone stale until Billy, ever the exhibitionist, shows them a way to spice up their sex life.

THE MAJOR AND THE MINERS: A Gay Historical Romance

1930s Australia: Two men from opposite ends of the social spectrum. Is love enough to overcome the obstacles between them?

THE GRAVY TRAIN: A Murder Mystery with Recipes

Someone on the train has an appetite for murder!

A TOUCH OF THE SON: A Gay Novel

Their secret passion will lead them to hell. Will they be able to find their way back?

ROMANCING THE BONE: Gay Romance Erotica

OMG! NOT ANOTHER GAY EROTICA ANTHOLOGY?

ROUGH & READY: Gay Tough Guy Erotica

YOUR BOYFRIEND IS HOT: Gay Cuckold Erotica

BEAR SKIN: Hot Gay Bear Erotica

THE MORE THE MERRIER: Gay Gangbang Erotica

THE BOY IS A BOTTOM: Gay Anal Erotica

COCK-EYED OPTIMISTS: Gay Romance Erotica

BABY, I'M NOT A MONSTER: Gay Vampire and Other Paranormal Erotica

CHRISTMAS CRACKER: Gay Erotica for the Holidays

BUTT BOYS: Gay Anal Erotica

HOW MUCH IS THAT DOGGIE IN THE WINDOW?

BACHELOR BOY

BAD-ASS BOYS

EVERYTHING'S COMING UP ROSES

SELECTED SHORT FICTION

Available as eBooks

LOVE WITH A SIDE ORDER OF PELICANS

CHRISTMAS IN JULY

BREEDING MY BOYFRIEND

NEW JOCK IN TOWN

BACHELOR BOY

SUMMER AT RAINBOW COVE

I WAS A MALE NYMPHO FOR THE FBI

HOW MUCH IS THAT DOGGIE IN THE WINDOW?

THE DAY OF THE CLIFFORDS

HE WON'T SEND ROSES

A RED ROSE BEFORE CRYING

PRIDE AND JOY

ROAD HUMP

THE GOOD, THE BAD, AND THE CUDDLY

THE GROOM CLOSET

TUNNEL VISION

HARD ON HIS HEELS

SPIN THE BOTTOM

THE NEW DAD'S CLUB

FOUR ON THE FLOOR

TAGGED BY THE TEAM

WANNA SHARE YOUR HUSBAND

For all Barry's titles please visit his page at: lydianpress.com

Lydian Press is dedicated to bringing you the finest GLBTQ erotic literature on the web.

Visit us on the web at:
http://lydianpress.com